Prais
bestselling author Mary Jo (Mrs.) Putney

∾

RWA Nora Roberts Lifetime Achievement Award
NJRW Career Achievement Award
Romantic Times Career Achievement Award
Two RITA Awards

∾

"Putney's writing is clear as crystal and smooth as silk."
—*Booklist*

"Mary Jo Putney is a gifted writer with an intuitive understanding of what makes romance work."
—*Jayne Ann Krentz*

BEWARE FAERY GIFTS

A Regency Fantasy Novella

M.J. PUTNEY

PANDAMAX
PRESS

COPYRIGHT

PANDAMAX
PRESS

～

FOREWORD

Beware Faery Gifts was originally published under the title *Dangerous Gifts* in an anthology called *Faery Magic* (named a Notable Book of the year by *Library Journal*) that also included stories by Jo Beverley, Barbara Samuel, and Karen Harbaugh. The stories were all Regency or Georgian, and we had so much fun that we did two more magical anthologies together, *Dragon Lovers* and *Chalice of Roses*.

My story here is about the danger of accepting gifts from faeries...

—Mary Jo Putney

PROLOGUE

LIQUID HARP NOTES floated down the wind, gentle as a dream. The faery lord listened with closed eyes as the music twined warmly around him. The harpist was a young mortal female, and she had played her haunting tunes in his wood many times. At first he had merely enjoyed the music. Then, when the winter chill kept her from the wood, he had realized how much more satisfying it would be to make the harpist his own. Then he would always have music.

When she returned to the wood in the spring, he had studied her and woven his plans. Today he would put them into motion. Impatient to begin, Ranulph of the Wood opened his eyes and set off toward the glade where the girl played her instrument with a power and passion that made the leaves and sunbeams dance.

At the edge of the glade, he paused in the shadows to study his quarry, Leah Marlowe. She sat on the trunk of a fallen tree, caressing the small Celtic harp like a lover as her fingers rippled out a tune that pierced the heart.

Slight of build with pale skin and straight brown hair, the girl was not a beauty even by mortal standards. Compared to a lady of Faerie, she was positively plain. Yet there was a sweetness about her, and she had a magical gift for music. He would have that sweetness and magic for himself. Beguiling her would be an easy task, for she was shy and lonely. Perhaps, if he was lucky, he would have her in his gilded lair this very night.

He smiled at the thought, and prepared to step into the glade.

"Why don't you leave the child alone?"

Jolted out of his reverie by the husky feminine voice, Ranulph whirled, his hand falling to the hilt of his sword. A scant two yards away, a female of unearthly beauty lounged gracefully against an oak.

She was of Faerie, of course, for few mortals could see him until he revealed himself. But her complexion was dusky, not the snow-pale hue of the Folk, and silken hair of raven-wing black floated around her shapely form and cascaded to her heels. Her garb was as exotic as her person, a length of shimmering fabric that wrapped around her in a most revealing way, exposing one flawless shoulder and slim bare arms circled with dozens of gilded bangles.

Ranulph's gaze went over her appreciatively. Even by the standards of Faerie, she was stunning. "What is your name? I've never seen a faery like you."

"My name is Kamana." She smiled with feline amusement. "Most assuredly you have seen no one like me, for none of my Folk have ever journeyed so far. I come from the other side of the world, from the land of Hind."

"India!" Ranulph said, intrigued. "So Faerie extends even there?"

"Faerie is everywhere, for we are of nature, not man." Kamana bent to pluck a sprig of woodruff, her bangles tinkling musically. "There are differences from land to land, of course.

The mortals of Hind reflect us, just as your Anglish humans reflect you."

"English," he corrected.

"As you wish, my lord." She crushed the woodruff stem, releasing a scent like new-mown hay. "And what is your name?"

"I am Ranulph of the Wood. How did you manage to come so far? Did you travel through Faerie?"

She shook her head. "No, for that is a dangerous shifting way, more perilous even than the lands of men."

"Surely the mortal world was even worse!" he exclaimed, appalled. "Such great spans of desert and sea would be lethal to one of the Folk."

"I traveled with a shipment of shrubs and flowers brought back by an Anglishman who had lived many years in Hind. Townley filled half a ship's hold with his specimens, letting in the sunlight when the weather was fair. It was near enough to a garden for me to survive." Kamana's eyes, a shade of dark gold as unique as the rest of her, darkened to pure night. "For eight long months, I dwelt in that hold as the ship ran before the winds and rolled between the seas. I know now what human hell must be!"

Ranulph nodded, understanding how wretched such confinement would be for one of the Fair Folk. "Why did you undertake such a perilous passage?"

She shrugged, her garment shimmering with the iridescence of a butterfly wing. "From curiosity. For amusement." Light sparked again in her slanted eyes. "For destiny, perhaps, Lord Ranulph."

"Destiny!" he snorted. "In this land, we forge our own fates."

"Or think you do," she said cryptically. "In Hind, we know that all beings dance to the measure of the weaver of the web, whether they recognize that or not." Her gaze went to the clearing, where the girl still played her harp, oblivious to the fact that she was observed. "The child plays exquisitely."

"It's hard to believe she is mortal," he agreed.

Kamana's eyes narrowed. "I suspect she has some faery blood in her. See the shimmer of magic when her fingers touch the strings?"

The cursed female was right. Irritated that she had seen what he had not, Ranulph said shortly, "Whatever her blood, soon she will be playing her music only for me."

"You mean to ensorcel her?" Kamana arched her dark brows. "In Hind, we cannot bind a mortal unless he or she consents to be placed in our power."

"The law is the same here." His possessive gaze went to the girl again. "I shall offer her the dearest wish of her heart. She will accept, and soon she will be mine."

Kamana frowned. "You shame yourself to enslave an opponent so unequal to you! She is but a child."

"She will be my consort, not my slave," he said brusquely.

A faint expression of distaste showed on Kamana's exquisite face. "Among my Folk, it is considered...vulgar to take mortals for mates. Oh, lying with them is all very well— indeed, it's a great pleasure. But for consorts, we keep to our own kind. Surely there are ladies of Faerie who would suit you better."

"In this land the Folk are of two types, those who live in courts and celebrate together, and the solitaries, like me." Voice clipped, Ranulph went on, "Oh, there are court ladies willing to come and share my bed for a night or two, but none would ever consider becoming consort to a solitary." He knew that for truth, because more than once he had invited one of the gilded court ladies to share his life, and been laughed at for his trouble.

There was flicker of brighter gold deep in her eyes. Then

she nodded gravely. "It is the same in my own land. But the price for a mortal to leave her own kind and dwell in Faerie is high."

"So are the rewards." He moved his hand impatiently. "Begone, lady of Hind! I've work to do." He turned his back and moved into the glade. But behind him he heard laughter, and perhaps a trace of mockery.

CHAPTER 1

EYES CLOSED and small body rocking gently, Leah flowed with her music, losing herself in the pulsing rhythms of the harp. In music, there was no loneliness or sorrow, only sweet abandon.

She came to the end of a long ballad and bent her head with a sigh. It was almost time to return home, and to drab reality.

Very near, someone cleared his throat. Her eyes flew open. To her surprise, a man of terrifying elegance stood right beside her. He was incredibly handsome, his immaculate London garb not concealing the strength of his tall frame.

Instantly tongue-tied, she clutched her harp and stammered, "A...are you lost, sir?"

He bowed, sweeping his hat so low that it brushed the verdant turf. "Not in the least. I came to find you, Leah, and in that I have succeeded." His hair was golden, and when he straightened she saw that his eyes were a startling true, clear green.

She held the harp even more closely. "Why would you want to find me, sir?"

"I have often heard you playing your harp in my wood,

Leah. Because of the pleasure I've had from your music, I've come to give you a gift."

"They are not your woods," she said politely. "This land is part of Marlowe Manor, so it belongs to my father, Sir Edwin Marlowe."

The stranger smiled, a chancy light dancing in his eyes. "There are many kinds of ownership, Leah. The wood is mine in a way that it will never belong to Sir Edwin."

"I have not given you leave to be free with my name." She stood, her harp in her arms, and began to edge away warily away.

"I shall not harm you, Leah," he said as if reading her mind. "I desire only to grant your dearest wish."

Her mouth twisted. The late child of elderly parents, she had known she was an unwanted nuisance before she learned to walk. If she had been pretty and charming, she might have won her parents' hearts, but she had been as nondescript as the faded wallpaper in the hall. She had caused no trouble, and in return was treated with absent-minded courtesy. And this man spoke of granting her dearest wish! She wanted to be lovely and lovable, but even a London gentleman could not give her that.

"Ah, but I can," he said softly. "I am Ranulph of the Wood, a lord of Faerie. I can give you beauty so great that it will bring all mortal men to their knees. Wealth, fame, the love of heroes —you can have whatever, or whomever, you most desire."

She gaped at him. He was mad; there could be no explanation. Or perhaps she was merely dreaming.

"This is no dream." Ranulph took her right hand and raised it to his lips, pressing a cool kiss on her tense fingers. "It is a sign of your own magical gift of music that you can see me. Usually only sorcerers or simple country people can see the Folk, but sometimes artists and poets and musicians can also."

She pulled her hand away, beginning to wonder if by some wild chance this encounter could be real. The woods around her had always had an uncanny reputation, and the villagers avoided the area. Leah came to this glade to play because the music inside her was always most powerful here. "If you're a faery, prove it."

He shook his head sadly. "So skeptical, you modern mortals." He reached inside his coat and drew out a small looking glass. Then he extended it to her, his fingers trailing sparkling light. "See what you might be."

Leah looked into the glass, and almost passed out with shock. The image revealed was stunningly beautiful. Her mousy brown hair had become a marvelously thick, glossy mane streaked with sun-kissed blondness, while her nondescript, gray-green eyes were a striking shade of green. Her fair skin seemed almost to glow and her features had been refined to exquisite perfection. Yet eerily, the face was still hers.

The image shimmered, and suddenly it showed plain Leah Marlowe again. She gave a small whimper of protest at the loss of that vision of loveliness.

Ranulph lowered the mirror. "You can look like that, Leah. Say the word, and you will be able to go to London as an acclaimed beauty and take your choice of the finest gentlemen in Britain. You shall be declared a diamond of the first water. Become a duchess, perhaps, if that is what you wish."

"Such beauty would be wasted, for my parents would never take me to town." She tried to sound as if that deprivation did not bother her.

"There is more than one way to get to London."

Nervously she brushed back her hair, torn between disbelief and the palpable reality of her surroundings. The scents and sounds were of the familiar glade, and this Ranulph seemed as genuine as anyone she'd ever seen.

He smiled at her. "I am as real as you, though of a different nature."

He could also read her mind, which certainly supported his claim of being a faery. Warily she said, "You will give me so much simply because you've enjoyed my music?"

He gave a world-weary shrug. "You would also have to make some small future payment when I come to claim it."

She looked into his eyes, and suddenly believed that he was what he said, for there was something deeply alien in those green depths. Something ancient beyond words, even though his face was that of a man in the prime of his life.

"You want my soul," she said flatly. "There are stories of faeries stealing human souls because they have none of their own."

He laughed, as charming as the London gentleman he resembled. "You mustn't believe all those old tales. I have no interest in stealing your soul."

"Do you have a soul of your own?"

"I really don't know," he said thoughtfully. "The Folk live so long that the issue is not one I have considered. But I assure you that even if I lack a soul myself, I wouldn't know how to take yours, much less what to do with it."

Oddly, she believed him, even though this conversation was increasingly bizarre. "If not my soul, what would you want of me?"

He shrugged again. "I haven't decided."

Relieved to have a good reason to deny his gift, she said, "I can't possibly agree to something when I don't know the price to be paid."

She started to move away, but he caught her gaze with his. "When the time comes, I will give you three choices. I shall not ask for your soul or your life—my oath upon it," he said with cool deliberation. "Surely one of the choices offered will be something you shall not mind paying."

She hesitated, knowing she should leave, but unable to deny the mesmerizing lure of his green eyes. Trying to sound firm, she said, "No."

"You will be beautiful beyond words, Leah," he said softly. "Men will offer you their love, their wealth, their devotion. Heroes will lay their glory at your feet. You will be the most envied woman in the land."

To be loved, not alone. To be beautiful. She thought of that entrancing image in the mirror, and wanted to weep with longing.

Seeing that she was weakening, he said in a voice like honey, "I am not asking you to do evil, my dear girl. You have blessed me and my wood with your music. I simply want to give you a token of my gratitude. But according to the laws of my world, a faery cannot give a gift without some kind of an exchange. I say again, you will not have to forfeit your soul, or your life. You'll have three choices, Leah. Surely one will be the merest trifle for you to pay."

Treacherously, he raised the mirror again. The beautiful Leah was there, gowned in silk and lace instead of the drab, worn gown that the real Leah wore.

She looked into the eyes of her false image, trying to find evil or corruption. But she saw only herself, happy and beautiful. She ran her tongue over dry lips. To be lovely and loved....

With sudden reckless passion, she knew that she wanted love at any price. Even if she possessed it for only for a handful days, it would be better than the emptiness of her present existence. She drew a ragged breath. "Very well, Lord Ranulph. I will accept your offer of beauty and love. In return you will give me three choices of repayment, and will not ask for my mortal life or immortal soul."

His smile was dazzling, though his teeth were rather... pointed. She reminded herself firmly that cats had pointed teeth, and she was very fond of them. She still missed her old tabby, gone since the last winter.

With a glitter of light, a silver dagger materialized in his hand. As she stiffened, he coolly sliced the center of his left palm. A crimson line appeared. Before she could retreat, he caught her hand and made a matching cut in her palm. Strangely, even though blood formed along the wound, it did not hurt. Rather, it stung like ice against bare flesh.

He pressed his palm to hers. "Flesh to flesh, blood to blood, a faery bond is formed." His voice was soft, but in his piercing eyes was a wild, alien light.

She gasped and snatched her hand away. "What wicked magic have you done?"

Lord Ranulph smiled, a sophisticated London gentleman again. "It was the merest formality, my dear girl." He took her hand again, but this time he only bowed elegantly over it. "You will not regret this, Leah. Go home now, and enjoy the blessings of faery magic." He straightened and gestured across the glade at a bird perched on a branch. "Very soon you shall take flight like that turtle dove."

Her gaze followed the fluttering wings as the dove rose into the air. She watched until it soared out of sight among the trees, then turned back to Ranulph of the Wood.

He was gone, leaving not so much as a single footprint or broken blade of grass.

She drew a dazed breath and sank onto the fallen tree trunk. The cool wind slid over her heated face. Had the faery vanished, or never existed?

She looked at her left hand, but there was no trace of a cut. Pressing her cheek against the silky wood of her harp, she bent her head and closed her eyes. The encounter must have been some sort of dream. She had dozed, and dreamed of a magical offer that would bring her happiness. She'd had many such fanciful daydreams as a child, though never one so realistic.

Face taut, she stood and slung her harp over her shoulder. Now she was grown and knew that happiness did not come with the swish of a magic wand—or the slash of a magical dagger. The reality was that eventually she would inherit a comfortable independence and would never want for anything. She was a fortunate woman, for she did not need a husband or children or passionate, romantic love.

It had only been a dream.

Leah entered the manor house quietly and headed for the stairs. Her dream of Faerie had delayed her, and she barely had time to change before dinner.

Then her mother called, "Leah, dear, come in here, please."

"Yes, Mother." Leah smoothed a hand over her wind-whipped hair, then slung the harp as far behind her as possible. Her parents approved of her skill on the pianoforte, but they had never understood her strange passion for a common, old-fashioned harp.

The instrument had been the gift of the old Irishman who had been her father's forester until his death the previous winter. McLennan had taught her to play. He'd also filled her ears with tales of the Faery Folk, of how they loved music and how he himself had once spent a midsummer's night listening to the wild melodies of faery harpers. Then he'd nod and say that Leah had the same gift.

The memory relaxed her. It was McLennan's tales that had produced that strange—dream? Hallucination? A faery in the woods! She must have been mad.

Leah entered the morning room, where her mother reclined on a brocade sofa. "Do you need something, Mother? Your shawl, perhaps?"

Lady Marlowe, gray-haired and chronically vague, but still retaining some of the frail prettiness of her youth, looked up from the letter in her hands. "'Tis the most extraordinary thing. This has just come from your father's cousin, Lady Wheaton. She's one of your godparents, you know."

Leah nodded. Her ladyship had sent her goddaughter an elaborate silver christening cup twenty-one years before. That was the extent of their relationship.

"Andrea wishes for you to join her in London for the Little Season. She's a widow, you know, and she's decided that it would be amusing to present a girl to society."

Leah gasped. "London—me? I...I would have no idea how to get on."

"Nonsense," her mother said reprovingly. "You're well-bred and a very handsome girl. You shall be a great success. Your father and I have often discussed taking you to London, but..." Her shrug delicately explained that such a project had been beyond her strength.

Leah scarcely noticed, for she was stunned by the remark that she was a very handsome girl. Apart from an occasional sigh after studying her daughter's unprepossessing countenance, or perhaps a remark that it was a pity Leah resembled her father's side of the family, Lady Marlowe had always been silent on the subject of her daughter's looks.

Weakly Leah said, "I have no clothing suitable for fashionable society."

"You'll need a new wardrobe, of course. Andrea shall select it for you." Lady Marlowe refolded the letter neatly. "Since you will be taking few of your own clothes, it won't take long for you to pack. You can leave tomorrow morning. Andrea is most anxious to welcome you."

"As you wish, Mother." Still dazed, Leah left the morning room and headed upstairs to her room. In her—dream—Ranulph had said that there was more than one way to get to London. Could he have arranged this visit?

Absurd!

Then she passed the gilt-framed pier glass that hung in the upper hall, and came to a dead stop, as stunned as if she had been hit with a hammer. The image in the mirror was that of the beautiful, faery-touched Leah that Ranulph had shown her. But now she could see all of herself. Her hair was a sensual, tawny mane and her figure was alluringly petite instead of merely thin.

She touched the reflection with shaking fingers, half expecting it to vanish like an image in a pond, but there was no change. As her mother had said, she was a remarkably handsome girl. No, more than that. She was beautiful. Achingly, heart-stoppingly beautiful. Even in her worn gown, she looked like a princess. No man would be able to resist her.

Yet as she had noticed earlier, she was still herself. Each of her features was much as before, but now refined to perfection. Her fair complexion, always good, was now flawless. Her formerly average gray-green eyes had become a riveting shade of green—exactly like those of Ranulph of the Wood.

Involuntarily she glanced down at her left palm. The sunlight revealed a faint, silvery line across the center, exactly where Ranulph had drawn his dagger.

Her hand dropped. With eerie calm, she accepted that Ranulph had been real, and she had pledged herself to an unholy bargain. What she would have to pay when the time came? For now, it didn't matter. As her eyes drank in the sight of her new self, she knew that what she had received was worth an uncertain price.

She tore herself away from the pier glass and hurried to her bedroom in the east wing. As soon as she closed the door, she looked into her own mirror, half afraid it would reflect the drab image of her old self. But it was the beautiful Leah who looked back, and who reflected Leah's joyous laughter.

Exuberant, she set down her harp, then whirled across the room in a mad dance. She was beautiful and going to London and she would have admirers by the score. She would enjoy the attention, then love and marry the best of her suitors. Everything she had silently yearned for would be hers.

Still laughing, she threw open her casement windows and leaned out. "Look out, London, here I come!"

Leah did not expect a response, but a lady-like "Meow" sounded from very close at hand. She glanced to her left in surprise.

Perched daintily on the branch of a tree that grew near Leah's window was a magnificent cat with long silky black hair and golden eyes. It was quite unlike any other cat Leah had ever seen, but quite in keeping with the events of the day. "Good day," Leah said courteously. "Are you a magical faery feline?"

The cat compressed itself like a coiled spring, then made an amazing leap that took it all the way to Leah's window. After landing lightly on the sill, it rubbed its cheek against Leah's arm, purring powerfully.

Leah stroked the cat's back. The splendid black fur was silky soft. "What a beautiful lady you are. You couldn't be anything but a lady."

The cat raised her aristocratic head and regarded Leah with huge golden eyes that seemed as intelligent as those of any human. Leah blinked. Perhaps this really was a faery being.

Feeling absurd, she asked, "Did Ranulph send you to watch me?"

Making a disdainful feline sound, the cat jumped from the sill into Leah's room, glided across the carpet, then leaped onto the bed. There she circled thrice around before settling down to sleep in a furry ball.

"You certainly believe in making yourself at home," Leah said with amusement. She sat on the bed by the cat and began petting again. "I'd love to keep you, but I'm sure that you already have a home." Though she could not imagine who in the neighborhood might own such a rare and obviously valuable cat. Leah knew every pet for miles around, and none of them were remotely like this lovely creature.

The cat purred ecstatically as Leah's fingers found the sensitive spot under her throat. Leah asked, "What shall I call you?"

The cat opened her eyes for a moment. As her gaze met Leah's, a word formed in Leah's mind. Half convinced she was ready for Bedlam, Leah asked, "Is your name Shadow?"

Radiating satisfaction, the cat closed her eyes again and tucked her nose under the magnificent plumy tail.

Leah was definitely ready for Bedlam. Nonetheless, she hummed with pleasure as she changed her clothing for dinner.

All was chaos at Marlowe Manor the next morning. Ranulph drifted across the grounds and took refuge in the shade of a topiary hedge as he watched the preparations for sending Miss Leah to London. First the massive travel coach lumbered out of the carriage house. Then a footman brought out a small trunk of the young lady's clothing. Ranulph was glad to see that she was not taking much; he'd never been impressed by her wardrobe. Luckily that would be improved in London. And of course when she was his, he'd garb her in moonbeams and faery silks.

Leah herself appeared, looking harassed and a little frightened to be leaving home for the first time in her life. In her arms was the case that held her harp. Behind her trailed the elderly maid who would accompany her to London, then return with the coach. Last of all came her parents, dutifully bidding their daughter good-bye.

Ranulph studied Leah hungrily. Mortals had such enticing vitality. The addition of faery glamour had made her lovely indeed. But his magic was limited by the fact that she was not yet bound to him; all he could do was maximize the features she had.

When she was fully his, he'd be able to alter her appearance at will. Make her tall, perhaps, or voluptuous, or give her the silvery blond hair of a faery queen. It would be like having his own private harem. Perhaps he'd give her black hair that swirled and danced about her heels. Though he'd never fancied black hair, it might be a pleasant change since most ladies of Faerie were blond.

Leah was on the verge of climbing into the coach when a fluffy black cat streaked by her and leaped into the vehicle. Leah removed the cat. It was back inside before she'd straightened up.

Ranulph laughed as he watched the ensuing battle. Cats were uncanny beasts who wandered freely between Faerie and the mortal world. This one had obviously been drawn by the scent of magic.

A footman caught the cat, only to have it wiggle loose in the blink of an eye. After the beast was removed from the coach again, Leah and the maid were hastily shut inside before the cat could rejoin them. It countered with a magnificent leap onto the coach, landing on the seat next to the driver.

Since the cat was clearly set on going to London, Leah wisely surrendered and opened the carriage door, The creature lightly sprang into the coach beside her and curled up daintily on the seat. Lady Marlowe suggested that if her daughter must take that *feline*, at least put it in a basket. Leah smiled and said that wouldn't be necessary. Ranulph was pleased by her insight and flexibility; she'd do well when he brought her into Faerie.

With a mighty lurch, the coach set off. The Marlowes and the servants who had come to send the little miss off returned to their normal activities. Only Ranulph was left to watch the coach disappear around the bend in the drive.

He felt a surge of sadness, coupled with flashing impatience. Goddess, but he wanted her! But he must wait, give her time to become addicted to the power of her beauty, and to become infatuated with some mortal man. Then she'd be ripe for the plucking. To move too quickly would be to risk losing her. He'd realized the day before that she could not be rushed.

Briefly he considered Lady Kamana. An odd creature, but amusing and quite attractive in her foreign way. Perhaps he could use her as a distraction for the next long weeks. But she'd left the wood; he'd felt the moment when she slipped away, as he sensed everything that happened in his territory. In her desire to explore her new land, Lady Kamana could be anywhere by now.

He wondered what the other Folk would think of her. Sometimes the Folk could be cruel to those who were different, as he knew from hard experience.

The idea struck when he was returning to the wood. Why not go to London himself? The place was a great sink of dead stone and teeming humankind, but there were parks with enough greenery for him to endure a visit. Not only would he be able to see Leah, but other sights as well. It had been long since he'd traveled to London.

He tried to remember just how long. That fellow Henry, the one with the six wives, had been king then. The city would be much changed. Probably not for the better, but still, a visit would be interesting, and would fill the waiting time.

He'd wait a bit before going. Give Leah time to adjust. With luck, she might be ready for him sooner than he expected.

Steps light, he glided into the welcoming depths of the wood.

CHAPTER 2

Shadow in her arms, Leah descended wearily from the coach in front of Lady Wheaton's immense London townhouse. It was late afternoon, and two days of rattling around the inside of a badly sprung vehicle had left her exhausted and depressed. She was so far from home. Why had she willingly gone among strangers? She and her party had spent the previous night in a coaching inn, and the stares of the men there had been positively rude. Even with her maid and coachman near, she had felt nervous.

Dispiritedly she followed her maid up the steps, then waited for admission to the house. When an elderly butler opened the door, she said, "I am Miss Marlowe. Lady Wheaton is expecting me."

The butler gaped at her before giving a little shake, like a dog after a bath. "This way, miss," he said, in control again. "Her ladyship wishes to see you immediately."

Cat still in her arms, Leah followed the servant upstairs to a small, richly decorated boudoir. A tall woman of middle years reclined on a brocade-covered chaise longue, a letter in her hands and a small dog curled up at her feet. Solemnly the butler announced, "My lady, Miss Marlowe has arrived."

Lady Wheaton lowered the letter and looked up. Dressed in the height of fashion, she had strong, handsome features and an air of command.

Leah curtsied as well as she could with a substantial cat draped over one shoulder. "Good day, Lady Wheaton. It is so kind of you to invite me here to London."

For a moment Lady Wheaton stared with the stunned expression Leah was becoming used to now that her appearance had changed. Then her ladyship rose and came forward, the small dog at her heels. "How lovely you are! Your mother was too modest in singing your praises." She studied Leah with interest. "You shall be a great success. I guarantee it. But my dear child...a cat?"

Leah, who had begun to revive under the admiration, blushed. "I'm sorry, my lady. Shadow would not be left behind."

Her godmother frowned. "Neither Rex nor I are at all fond of cats."

A sharp canine yip identified Rex. The dog bounded toward Leah, looking ready to chase or eat the feline invader.

Shadow jumped from Leah's arms and stared at Rex. The dog skidded to a stop. Then he whined and flattened his belly to the floor, all the fight gone out of him.

The cat stalked forward, gaze locked with the dog's, until their noses touched. After a moment of whimpering panic, Rex gave a kind of sigh and relaxed.

Shadow turned to Lady Wheaton and began to strop her ankles, purring vociferously. Her ladyship's first expression of distaste vanished almost immediately. "It's quite a friendly creature, isn't it?" She bent and patted the cat's head, as if Shadow was a dog. "And rather pretty, for a cat."

Leah almost laughed as she watched Shadow charming her hostess.

Lady Wheaton straightened. "Since Rex doesn't seem to object, I suppose there's no harm in having the creature here, but don't allow it to scratch my furniture."

Clearly her ladyship knew nothing of cats, or she would not have the foolish idea that one could exact obedience from one. Still, Shadow hadn't scratched anything yet, and she seemed to have a clear sense of which side her bread was buttered on. Meekly Leah said, "Yes, Lady Wheaton. She is a very good cat."

"Call me Aunt Andrea," Lady Wheaton said warmly. "You must be tired. You'll want to take supper in your room. I shall have a tray sent up. Then you must get a good night's sleep, for tomorrow we'll be off to the modiste to order your wardrobe. I am giving my autumn ball next week. It will be the perfect occasion to present you."

She slowly circled Leah. "Wait until Lady Hill sees you," she said with satisfaction. "The whole spring season she went on insufferably about how beautiful her daughter Mary is, but you quite put the girl in the shade. Presenting you will be a great triumph for me. You'll be the belle of the season."

A little dismayed, Leah collected Shadow and withdrew. She hadn't known that she would be used to score points for her godmother in what looked like a long-term rivalry. Still, she supposed it was harmless enough.

As she settled into an airy, attractive bedchamber, she turned her thoughts to the far more pleasant prospect of a new wardrobe.

∿

The footman handed Leah into the carriage. She collapsed on the seat opposite her godmother with a sigh. "I had no idea how fatiguing it is to be fashionable. It's been three days now of shopping and fittings, being pinched and pinned." She glanced out the window as the carriage began to move. "May I remove the veil? It is not comfortable on such a warm day."

"Wait until we are away from Bond Street," Lady Wheaton ordered. "I don't want to risk anyone seeing you in public before the grand presentation at my ball." She pursed her lips absently. "Instead of introducing you in the usual receiving line, I shall wait until most of the guests have arrived. Then we will make a grand entrance down the front staircase."

Leah suppressed a sigh, not sure she would like being so much the center of attention, but know it was her duty to cooperate with Lady Wheaton's plans. Luckily, she was becoming quite fond of her tart-tongued but generous-hearted godmother. "Very well, Aunt Andrea."

Still full of energy despite so much shopping, her godmother said, "It's time to start discussing potential husbands. There are several available royal dukes, of course, but they are an unreliable lot. I want better for you."

Thank heaven for that. Even Leah know that the unmarried royal dukes were fat, middle-aged, and chronically in debt. And from what she inferred from news stories, they were not very bright. She wanted to marry a man she could talk to. "I wouldn't want to be a duchess. Indeed, I would make a sad muddle of such a high rank."

"You simply must put a higher value on yourself, my dear," Lady Wheaton said briskly. "I've never known a beautiful woman who had so little confidence as you. In relations between the sexes, a woman's beauty is power. You must use yours to acquire the wealth and security that ensure a woman a comfortable life. Granted, the royal dukes are poor choices, but there is the Duke of Hardcastle. Much more handsome than any of the Hanovers, and in the market for a second wife."

Her brows drew together. "Hardcastle is the greatest prize in the Marriage Mart, but there is young Lord Wye—you could win him with a snap of your fingers." Grandly she demonstrated a snap. "If you like the military sort, there is Duncan Townley, who is a Peninsular hero and heir to his uncle's viscountcy. Not the best title or the richest man, but very dashing. Or if you prefer poets, there is Lord Jeffers. Not so handsome as Byron, nor so good a poet, but far wealthier and better behaved."

Before her godmother could continue, Leah said with alarm, "But which are *agreeable* men? Sure that is paramount when choosing a husband!"

"When enough wealth is involved, one scarcely needs to see one's husband after the heirs have been produced. A wife who has done her duty to her husband's family has enormous freedom," Lady Wheaton said with an airy wave of her hand. "To continue, it is as important to know who is not eligible is to know who is. Under no circumstances can you accept dances from the following."

For the rest of the ride, her ladyship rattled off more names and pungent descriptions of each gentleman's virtues or failings as a potential matrimonial partner. By the time they reached Wheaton house, Leah's head was aching in earnest. She went directly to her room and flopped onto the bed.

Shadow, who had been watching the passing scene from the window seat, jumped to the floor and came to join Leah on the bed. Leah cuddled the cat, grateful for the undemanding company. In a strange and disorienting city, she sometimes had the odd feeling that Shadow was her guardian angel.

Even more than her cat, she needed music. Her gaze went

to her harp, which sat silent in its case beside her wardrobe. She hadn't played since arriving in London; she had simply been too tired. Perhaps after dinner... No, drat it. A dancing master was coming to make sure that Leah was proficient in all the latest dances.

She sighed and her eyes drifted shut. In a few more days, she would be presented. Then she would be a belle, and it would all be worth it.

Monique, Lady Wheaton's French maid, was putting the last touches on Leah's coiffure when her ladyship herself appeared in Leah's bedroom. "The ballroom is full, and almost every man on my eligible list has arrived. It's time for your grand entrance, Leah." Lady Wheaton smiled, eyes dancing. "For the last week I've been dropping hints to friends about how beautiful my goddaughter is, so everyone is madly curious. Now stand up and let me look at you."

Leah stood obediently while her godmother examined her appearance, her shrewd gaze missing nothing. "You'll do, girl. You'll do."

"What I might do is faint," Leah said weakly.

"Nonsense. Look at yourself." Lady Wheaton drew Leah toward the mirror. "You're a warrior girded for war, armored in beauty to fight the great battle of the sexes."

"I thought I was in London for love, not war." Then Leah saw her image in the mirror and gasped, all other thoughts forgotten. Her tawny hair had been swept into an irresistible confection of shining curls, secured here and there with golden combs. In a fashionably low-cut gown with a gauzy overskirt studded with brilliants, she looked like an exquisite faery princess.

The thought made her flinch. In a sense, she *was* a faery princess, or perhaps a faery doll, decorated as a plaything to amuse a faery lord. Her gaze lingered on her reflection. She must give Lord Ranulph credit—when he came to collect his price, she would be unable to say that he had stinted on his part of the bargain. Shining hair, perfect complexion, alluring sylph-like figure—she had received beauty in full measure.

She glanced at Shadow, who was sitting on her haunches watching. The cat's golden eyes seemed to gleam with warmth and approval. Absurdly comforted by the cat's expression, Leah said, "I'm ready, Aunt Andrea."

Arm in arm, the two women left Leah's bedroom and descended the sweeping staircase into the vestibule that opened into the flower-filled ballroom. Leah felt as if she were wading into a river of sound as the roar of conversation clashed with the energetic playing of the musicians.

Halfway down the stairs, heads began turning toward Leah and her godmother. Silence fell, rippling from the vestibule into the ballroom. One man said reverently, "By Jove!" while another exclaimed, "She's a goddess!"

Guests in the ballroom began crowding into the vestibule. Before Leah's startled eyes, the area at the bottom of the stairs filled with people, their eyes fixed on her. Most of the expressions were stunned admiration, but here and there tight-lipped women resentfully analyzed the new competition.

Leah froze, wanting to run back upstairs, but the pressure of Lady Wheaton's grip kept her moving down. "I told you," her godmother whispered triumphantly. "Look at them! You'll be betrothed to a duke before the month is out, my girl."

They reached the bottom of the stairs and were instantly surrounded by men with avid eyes and lusting hearts. A tall, heavy-set fellow demanded, "An introduction please, Lady Wheaton!"

Beside him, a soulful gentleman said with a French accent, "A dance, mademoiselle, you must save me a dance."

A wide-eyed young man called out, "Your hand in marriage, my dear goddess. I shall make you Countess of Wye."

Other demands, other needs, chewed at her. Leah could feel the lust coming from the men like animal heat. They were tall, strong, closing in like wolves....

You wanted to be admired. The words formed in her mind, light and ironical. Lord Ranulph, perhaps, watching her in some strange faery way?

The faint mockery of the thought steadied her. Well, she *had* wanted admiration. She simply needed time to become accustomed to so much attention. Already that first rush of panic was retreating.

Lady Wheaton began making introductions and allotting her protégée's dances. Leah was more than willing to let her godmother handle such things. Her own energy was engaged simply in keeping her wits about her. A pity she had never attended a ball as her normal, mousy self. If she had, she would be better prepared. But of course, her normal mousy self had never been invited anywhere.

After the flurry of introductions, she was handed into the keeping of her first dance partner, Lord Wye, the young man who had virtually proposed before he'd even learned her name. He was one of the eligibles Lady Wheaton had described, which meant that he was possessor of a vast fortune and an impressive title.

Unfortunately, he possessed neither a chin nor conversation. Throughout their dance, he simply stared at Leah adoringly. She guessed that he was no older than she. She felt torn between sympathy for his shyness, and amusement at the way he blushed whenever she ventured a comment. The smile she offered him at the end of their quadrille reduced him to babbling incoherence.

Her next partner, the Duke of Hardcastle, was more articulate. He was in his middle thirties, a widower and man of the world who was at the top of Lady Wheaton's list of eligibles. He was quite a handsome man, and he made witty comments whenever the patterns of the dance brought them together. Altogether a good husband prospect, except that his hot, hungry gaze seemed to strip her naked.

Yet even though Hardcastle made her nervous, she felt a glow of triumph at the knowledge that he wanted her. No one had ever wanted her old, plain self.

She curtsied prettily at the end of the dance. 'Thank you, your grace. You are very kind."

"Kindness has nothing to do with it." His heavy lidded gaze studied her with searing intensity. "Until next time, Miss Marlowe."

He returned her to Lady Wheaton, who took advantage of an interval between dances to introduce Leah to some of the powerful women who ruled London society. Leah had recovered enough from her earlier nervousness to smile, curtsy, and acknowledge the introductions without stammering.

Her progress was followed by approving comments such as "What pretty manners the girl has," and "She does you credit, Andrea."

Leah was tempted to laugh. She was merely practicing the courtesy learned by any child the schoolroom, yet some of the women acted as if her behavior was unusual. That meant either that great beauties were often rude, or that Leah was getting more credit for good manners than a less beautiful girl would.

By the end of the long evening, she was enjoying every shred of admiration that came her way. Lady Wheaton was right—this was power. The warm gazes were balm after a lifetime of being ignored. Leah's simplest remarks were greeted with laughter, as if she was a great wit. Her every smile was received like a precious gift. Her dances were sought after as if they were the holy grail.

She had become a belle—and she loved it.

CHAPTER 3

By the end of a fortnight's social activity, Leah was universally acknowledged as the Beauty of the season. So many flowers had been delivered that every room of Wheaton House was perfumed with blossoms. She had started a collection of the poetry that had been sent to her. Half of the pieces came from the adoring Lord Jeffers, society poet and eligible bachelor. As Lady Wheaton had said, he wasn't the poet that Byron was, but the man did know how to turn a pretty phrase.

Resting in her room before preparing for a ball at the Duke of Hardcastle's famous mansion, Leah smiled over Lord Jeffers' latest effort, then tucked it away. The poet was quite charming, but in love with the idea of love rather than with her.

She relaxed into her wing chair, welcoming the interval of peace and quiet. There had been few such times in the last fortnight. "It's very exciting being a belle, Shadow, but I haven't fallen in love yet," she said with a sigh. "I haven't even met someone I *want* to fall in love with. Is there something wrong with me?"

The cat turned her head to Leah, for all the world as if she were listening. A thought appeared in Leah's mind. *You haven't met the right man.*

Leah was no longer surprised at such incidents. Admittedly all cats were rather fey, but she was half convinced that Shadow had been sent by Lord Ranulph as some sort of guardian. If witches had familiars, why not faeries?

A wordless note of disgust touched Leah's mind. She grinned at the cat, who was twitching her plumy tail with irritation. "Do you find that thought insulting? I'm sorry." She removed her harp from its case, then sat again and ran experimental fingers over the strings. The familiar singing notes made her smile with pleasure. She settled down to play seriously. Her fingers were a little stiff, but they loosened rapidly.

It seemed no time at all before Monique entered. The maid said, scandalized, "Mam'zelle, you should be dressing for the ball!"

Leah almost protested that she wanted to spend the evening playing, but stopped herself. She had come to London to find love. There would be time for music later.

The dance ended and the Duke of Hardcastle bent to kiss Leah's hand. "You waltz beautifully, Miss Marlowe. But of course, you are beautiful in all ways."

Flushed from the swirling dance, Leah inclined her head graciously. "A good waltz requires a good partner."

The duke's mouth curved in a predator's smile. "As witty as you are lovely."

It hadn't been that witty, but by this time Leah had become used to such exaggerated reactions. The duke tucked her gloved hand into the crook of his arm and continued, "The ballroom is very warm. Come into my garden for some fresh air."

Leah hesitated. He had called at Wheaton House several times, always claimed two dances at each event, and had taken her driving once. Aunt Andrea said that bets were being laid in the clubs that Leah would be the next duchess. Leah wasn't sure how she felt about that. Hardcastle cut an impressive figure and he was certainly a great catch, but he still made her nervous.

She needed to become better acquainted with him. "I should like some fresh air, your grace."

As he guided her across the crowded ballroom, Leah studied the other guests. She had assumed that in London she would make friends with other young women, as she had at home, but that hadn't happened. The really pretty girls were jealous, and the average ones avoided her. Remembering her own plain days, she guessed that they thought she was only interested in finding foils for her own beauty. The knowledge saddened her. She had not thought beauty would come at the price of friendship.

As the orchestra struck up a new dance, Hardcastle led Leah through the French doors. Several other couples were on the stone patio in plain view of the ballroom, so this must be proper. But when he steered her toward the steps that led into the dark garden, Leah balked. "My godmother said I should not be alone with a man."

His brows rose impatiently. "I am not *a man,* I am the Duke of Hardcastle! Lady Wheaton would approve entirely."

Before Leah could protest again, they were on a gravel path that led into the heart of the immense garden. It was pleasant to be surrounded by dark, shadowy trees and the scents of growing things rather than chattering ball guests and sweaty bodies. Leah relaxed, enjoying the cool air and the knowledge that she was

being escorted by one of England's greatest lords. This scene
would have been unimaginable a month ago. "Your garden seems
very lovely, your grace. I would like to see it in daylight sometime."

"Whenever you wish, my dear." There was an odd, rough
quality to his voice.

The tree-lined path led into an open space. Though the
night was moonless, there was just enough starlight to see the
outlines of a marble statue set in the middle of a gently
plashing fountain. Leah squinted at the statue, then blushed,
glad for the darkness. The sculpture appeared to be a naked
woman entwined most improperly with a swan.

Deciding that she had bent the rules of propriety far
enough, she said, "Please take me back, your grace. I'm beginning to feel cold."

"I'll keep you warm." The rough note she had heard before
was stronger, and suddenly his arms were around her and his
mouth grinding into hers. When she tried to utter a protest,
his thick tongue slid between her lips.

She gagged, feeling as if she would be physically ill. She
pushed against his chest, but managed only to pull her face
away from his revolting kiss. "Your grace, please!" she pleaded.
"You forget yourself."

"It's because of you, my sweet," he said hoarsely. His hand
slid down and he squeezed her buttock, pressing her hard
against his hot, obscenely swollen body. "You're the most
exquisite creature I've ever seen. You make me mad with
desire!"

Shocked by the unwanted intimacy, she snapped, "That's
not my fault!"

She tried to twist away, but he maintained his grip. One of
his groping hands caught her breast. Near hysteria, she gasped,
"Let me go or I'll scream!"

"For God's sake, don't make such a fuss," he said impatiently. "I wouldn't seduce you in my own garden if my intentions weren't honorable."

Before she could say that this was not seduction but rape, his mouth crushed down on hers again. She realized with horror that he was tugging at her skirt. Dear God, she would never be able to break free! He was too strong, too intent on having his way. And if he did, she would have no choice but to marry him.

In her mind, she heard the cool words *You wanted a beauty that would drive men mad.* Lord Ranulph again? But she hadn't wanted *this!*

Suddenly a hard voice snapped, "Let her go!"

The newcomer enforced his command by physically breaking the duke's hold on Leah. Panting for breath, she retreated several steps and tried to see her rescuer. In the darkness he was only a faceless shadow. Of middle height, perhaps, with broad shoulders—and wonderful timing.

"Damn you, sir, do you know who I am?" the duke snarled at the interloper.

"I believe so," was the icy reply. "You do yourself no credit, your grace."

"You criticize *me?*" Hardcastle exclaimed, incredulous. "How dare you interfere between a man and his affianced wife!"

"She looked like an unwilling woman to me," the other man retorted. "Was I wrong about that, miss?"

"Tell this lunatic that we're betrothed!" Hardcastle ordered.

Leah wanted to say that she wouldn't marry the duke if he were the last man in Christendom, but barely in time remembered that it would not be wise to humiliate a man so powerful. And, in fairness, he'd had no reason to think she would not accept an offer.

"Though I do not question your honorable intentions, your grace, you neglected to go through the formality of making an offer," she said carefully. "You do me great honor, but...but I do not think we would suit."

"Wouldn't suit!" Hardcastle said with disbelief. "A nobody like you is turning down the chance to become a duchess?"

"Yes," she said in a small voice.

His jaw dropped. Then his expression changed to disdain. "I thought you worthy to be my wife, but you're only a foolish, impertinent little girl! You're quite right. We would not suit at all. I shall tell your godmother to summon her carriage because you are not feeling well. And I suggest that in the future, you avoid your sly tricks that lead a man to misread your affections." He spun on his heel and stalked off.

Leah stood there, shaking, until her rescuer said gently, "You'd best sit down."

He guided her to a bench. She folded onto the cold stone. "Thank you," she said unevenly. "When we came out for air, I...I had no idea what he intended."

"It's a fair guess that a man who takes a girl into a dark garden is up to no good," her rescuer said dryly as he peeled off his coat and draped it over her shoulders. "I suggest that you accept no more such invitations unless you are in favor of accepting the gentleman's advances as well."

He had a really wonderful deep voice. As she gratefully wrapped the body-warmed fabric around her, she tried again to see his face, but couldn't. He was simply a silhouette against darker shadows. Wanting his good opinion, she said earnestly, "Truly, I did not encourage the duke's advances, despite what he said."

"Then I presume you are very beautiful," he said cynically.

"Wealthy men tend to believe they are entitled to beautiful women, and beautiful women tend to assume that they deserve wealth. It's a bargain that has existed since time immemorial, so perhaps the duke can be forgiven for misunderstanding."

"What nonsense," she retorted. "Marriage should be more about love than wealth and beauty."

"You are very young," he said, but his voice had softened.

Her mouth curved ruefully. "I suppose so. But I don't appreciate having that pointed out to me."

"Neither would I," he agreed. "If you're feeling well enough, allow me to escort you around the house. Your godmother should be waiting for you there."

Silently Leah rose and took his arm. It was firm and well-muscled beneath the linen of his shirt. Strength that had been used for protection, not assault. As they moved through the garden, she said, "I hope the duke does not choose to ruin me socially."

"He won't," her rescuer said confidently. "The situation reflects badly on him."

When they reached the side of the mansion, the flaring torches lining the driveway revealed Lady Wheaton waiting beside her carriage, her expression concerned. Though Leah would like to see her rescuer's face, she did not want it to be at the price of him seeing hers, not after what had happened.

She stopped and slipped off his coat. As she handed it to him, she said, "You have my deepest thanks, sir. And—please don't watch me go."

Understanding, he said with amusement, "Leaving us strangers in the night, with all embarrassment safely covered by the dark. But what if we meet again?"

"We'll pretend this never happened," she said firmly.

"As you wish." He executed a courtly bow, his shirt pale in the darkness.

She gave him a sweeping curtsy, hoping they would meet again under more normal circumstances. Then, head high, she crossed the soft lawn to her godmother.

Her rescuer watched her for a moment, unconsciously raising the coat to his face, as if seeking for a trace of her scent. Then he turned back to the dark garden, before she was so well-lit that he could not fail to identify her in the future.

Hidden in the deepest shadows of the garden, Ranulph watched Leah join her godmother, his faery sight giving him a cat's vision at night. He'd been in London for several days, exploring the great parks but always coming back to the dense patch of bushes and trees in the center of the square where Wheaton House stood. Hungrily his gaze followed as Leah climbed into the carriage. Goddess, but he tired of waiting!

His hand tightened on the hilt of his sword. If he had been closer tonight, he might have slain the duke when the drunken sot had attacked her. Luckily that other mortal had happened along in time to save Leah from harm. It would have enraged the powers of Faerie if Ranulph had killed the duke because of a mortal woman. Debts must always be paid, and those between Faerie and the mortal world weighed heavy indeed.

Intent on his thoughts, Ranulph spun about with dangerous alarm when a warm hand touched his wrist. His grip on his sword relaxed when he saw that he had been accosted by Lady Kamana, the Indian faery.

"You again," he said, voice cool though in truth he was pleased to see her. "I thought you would have joined one of the faery courts by now."

"Nay, my lord." She tossed her head. Her long black hair was pulled into a luxuriant silken rope, banded every six inches by a circlet of gold until the tip brushed the earth. "I will not choose a permanent home until I've seen more of your land."

He'd forgotten how richly purring her voice was. Instead of her Indian silks, she was garbed in the provocative evening gown of a grand London lady. Perversely, the English garments made her seem even more exotic.

"You've made your little country girl very beautiful," she observed.

"You recognized her?" he said, surprised.

"Of course. You could not have made her outward appearance so beautiful if it did not reflect her soul. She is young as only mortals can be young, but her heart is good, and music runs through her like pure fire. Otherwise the faery glamour you laid on her would be a pale thing, fit only to convince mortals."

"Mortals are easily deceived," he said dryly. "I've made her the toast of London, but the foolish girl has not yet fallen in love, and I cannot ask my price until she does."

"Patience, Lord Ranulph. She will find the love of her life soon." A smile touched her voice. "Very soon."

Ranulph frowned. "Do your Folk see the future clearly? I can sense it sometimes, but not with any detail."

"When I concentrate, I can patterns of destiny like silver threads that run through time and space," Kamana said slowly. "They touch each other and create shining webs of love and hate and friendship."

"You can see Leah bonded to me?" Ranulph asked urgently. He'd sensed that he would soon be sharing his domain with another, but desire might be distorting his intuition. "She will be my consort?"

"Never fear, my lord. I see your thread intersecting that of your consort, forming a knot that will bind you together for eternity, or near enough." Kamana drew the heavy rope of her hair through her fingers, absently toying with the gold bangles that circled it. "Like all gifts, mine is a mixed blessing. I followed my own thread of destiny here, not knowing how close it would come to destroying me."

"You said the passage was difficult," he said as he imagined the months of confinement on shipboard.

She was silent for a long moment, her habitual shimmering vivacity stilled. "Even more difficult than I told you when we first met. At the start of the voyage, there was not enough of nature living on that ship. The mortal who was bringing the specimens back to England found me dying among his shrubs. He understood my malady, though I could say little, and demanded that the ship stop at a small tropical island. Days we stayed there, and I recovered my strength among the flowers and palms. When the ship continued, the mortal brought more greenery into the hold to sustain me for the rest of the journey."

"But he extracted a price from you," Ranulph said flatly. "It is ever the way of mortals to extract treasure from the Fair Folk when they have us in their power."

She flashed a smile in the darkness, shimmering again. "Aye, he asked a price, but not for himself. Merely to preserve his beloved nephew from death in battle, then find the boy a good mate. 'Twas not a price I mind paying."

"You were fortunate."

"I merely followed destiny's thread." She swept a perfect English curtsy. "Good night, my lord. I intend to stay in London for a time, so we shall meet again."

He bowed, then vanished into the shadows of the duke's garden.

Kamana stood and watched him leave, her inner vision studying the silver thread of his destiny.

CHAPTER 4

LADY WHEATON AT HER SIDE, Leah entered the Duke of Candover's ballroom with the graceful confidence that came to her naturally now. She had recovered from her encounter with the Duke of Hardcastle, and never let herself be caught alone by any of her other admirers. She had also improved her flirting, which made it easier to control the men who flocked around her. Flirting was a game, enjoyable in itself and also good at keeping people at precisely the distance one wanted them.

Lady Wheaton murmured, "Brace yourself, my dear, you've been seen."

Already men were flocking toward them. Most Leah knew, though a few were strangers drawn like moths to the flame. Several of them immediately demanded introductions from Lady Wheaton. Lord Wye planted himself in front of Leah and bowed. "You are in exceptionally fine looks tonight, Miss Marlowe."

"Thank you," she said with a friendly smile. She had already turned down three proposals from Lord Wye, but he had not given up yet.

Lord Jeffers intoned, "She walks in beauty, like a swallow's flight." He hesitated. "That's the first line of my new poem, but I'm not sure I've got the right phrase yet."

Leah touched his hand. "I'm sure you will," she said warmly. Then she turned so Lady Wheaton could make introductions. In the last weeks Leah had mastered easy social intercourse. In fact, she'd learned that beauty made almost all things easy.

Yet she was no closer to finding someone to love. The most attractive men she had met were those who were happily married, like her newly wed host, the Duke of Candover. Wanting nothing from her, such men were relaxed and charming companions.

At every social function she attended, she looked for the man who had rescued her from the Duke of Hardcastle, but without success. Instead of a guest, might he have been a servant, perhaps a gardener? She wanted to kick herself for running away in embarrassment that night instead of making his acquaintance. Ah, well, he was probably married and unavailable.

Leah had just returned from waltzing with a portly baronet when Lady Wheaton murmured behind the cover of an opened fan, "Captain Duncan Townley has just arrived. He doesn't go out socially very much, so he's the only one of my eligibles that you haven't met." She tapped her lips with the fan reflectively. "Since no one else has taken your fancy, perhaps he will. Half the women in London dote on him. A hero of Waterloo, you know, and heir to a viscount."

Leah glanced toward the door, then caught her breath involuntarily. The man who had just entered was stunning, the epitome of the bold, dashing hero who would make any woman's knees melt. Though not exceptionally tall, his lithe, broad-shouldered form radiated intense virility. A lock of dark wavy hair fell over his forehead as he surveyed the ballroom with hooded eyes. Leah tried to estimate his age. Not old, though, certainly under thirty. Awed, she whispered, "He's magnificent."

For an instant, she thought that he had noticed her. Then her view was blocked by women crowding forward to see him. She understood perfectly. In fact, she had to suppress a mad desire to walk up to Duncan Townley, link her arms around his neck, and announce that she was his destiny.

Such foolishness! Or was it? There was magic in her life now. Could Ranulph have sent her to London to meet Duncan Townley? The faery lord had said that she could command the love of heroes if she wished.

Smiling at her protégée's reaction, Lady Wheaton said, "Shall I introduce you?"

"Not yet. I must go to the ladies' retiring room and fix my hair." More nervous than she had been since the night of her presentation, Leah made her excuses to her circle of admirers and left. But instead of returning to the ballroom after checking her appearance, she detoured to the music room, which was blessedly empty.

She dropped onto the bench in front of the pianoforte and forced herself to breathe slowly. She must be calm when her godmother introduced her to Duncan Townley. With a man like that, who could have any woman, she would need every iota of her beauty, and charm as well. Nor could she appear too eager. She'd learned enough of men in the last weeks to know that many were captivated by a woman who seemed unattainable.

Her gaze went to the keyboard of the pianoforte. Unable to resist it, she stripped off her gloves and began to play, keeping the sound soft so that it would be inaudible in the ballroom. Mozart soothed her, reminding her of who she really was. Some days she feared that she was in danger of losing herself.

By the end of her first piece, she was so caught up in the music that she went immediately into Beethoven's "Moonlight Sonata." The knot of tension that had been part of her since coming to London dissolved. Eyes closed, she played by touch, gently rocking back and forth as her hands coaxed the divine melodies from the instrument.

At the end she sighed with happiness, head bowed as her hands stilled on the keyboard. Then the sound of clapping hands startled her from her reverie.

Her lids snapped open. To her shock, Duncan Townley was standing in the doorway applauding. Their gazes met for a charged moment. In his eyes she saw the same kind of intense interest that she felt for him.

He entered the music room with a panther-like smoothness that riveted her attention. "So this is where you've been hiding, fair lady," he said in a voice like deep, rich chocolate. "I saw you across the ballroom earlier, but you vanished before I could find you. I've been looking ever since." He halted beside the pianoforte. "You play extraordinarily well."

Leah's heart began to beat in triple time. The voice, the height and build—this was the man who had rescued her from the Duke of Hardcastle. "Thank you," she said, amazed at how steady her voice sounded. "You're Duncan Townley, and I am Leah Marlowe. Since my godmother intended to introduce us, we can now say that the formalities have been duly performed."

As soon as she spoke, his brows drew together in puzzlement. He must find her voice familiar also. How foolish of her to think that it would be possible to pretend their first meeting had never happened. She continued, "Besides, we have already met, in the garden of Hardcastle House. I am very much in your debt, Captain Townley."

"So it was you!" he exclaimed. "With your voice like singing bells." His gaze was almost fierce in its intensity. "Hardcastle's behavior was despicable—but I understand better now why he forget himself as he did."

Leah blushed, and wished that she hadn't. With this man, she cared about the impression she made. Cared desperately. He was glorious, the most attractive male creature she'd ever seen, except for Lord Ranulph, who was too alien to affect her heart.

Dear God, Duncan Townley couldn't be faery, could he? Her gaze shot up as she looked to see if his eyes were the same emerald green that showed in her own mirror. She exhaled with relief when she saw that they were a rare and striking transparent gold. Not green, thank heaven.

She must say something before he decided that she was an idiot. Casting about for a topic of conversation, she said, "My godmother says you are a hero of Waterloo."

Wrong topic. His golden eyes darkened. "I simply did my duty. There were many heroes that day, and too many of them are now dead."

The tan skin tightened over his face, revealing the fine line of a newly healed scar over his sculptured cheekbone. She guessed that it had been made by the slice of a saber. He might have been killed or blinded, but instead, the scar actually enhanced the rugged masculinity of his appearance.

The thought of him being wounded brought the reality of war to her as newspaper stories never had. On impulse, she stood and lightly touched the scar. Since her gloves were still off, there was an intimate contact of skin to skin. "I'm sorry," she said softly. "Surely it is bitter to lose so many of your friends, and then be acclaimed when they have been forgotten."

The warmth returned to his eyes. With utter simplicity, he turned his head and kissed the palm of her hand. "Thank you for understanding."

The touch of his lips sent fire shivering through her, warming deep places that she had not known existed. This was what she had longed for, she realized dazedly. The first tentative recognition between two souls that, God willing, would lead to love.

Without haste she lowered her hand. "I should return to the ballroom. My godmother would not be happy to learn that I was alone with a man." She made a face. "You know what happened the last time."

His brows arched. "Do you think I am like the Duke of Hardcastle?"

She considered flirting to keep him at a distance, but decided that it was already too late for that. "No. You are unlike anyone I have ever met."

For a moment, there was an expression that seemed almost like pain in his golden eyes. Then he smiled. "You're right that it is time to return to the ballroom. The next dance is a waltz, and you will dance it with me."

The thought of being held in his arms sent a delicious shiver through her, but she shook her head regretfully. "I'm sorry, this waltz is spoken for." She lifted her fan from the pianoforte and studied the sticks, where she had written the names of her partners. "Sir Amos Rowley, I believe."

"What a pity that you lost your fan." Duncan plucked the fragile object from her hand, then folded it neatly and tucked it inside his coat. "I shall gallantly volunteer to see that you are not forced to sit out this dance."

Her mouth curved. "I shall miss that fan," she said as she drew on her gloves again. "It was a gift from my godmother."

"I foresee that I will miraculously find it later." He placed her hand on his arm. "Naturally I must call on you tomorrow to return your fan. In gratitude, you will grant me a drive in the park."

She laughed buoyantly, loving the feeling of being swept along by the force of his interest. Why was it that behavior that might irritate her in another man simply made him more attractive? She set the thought aside for another day. What mattered now was this moment, and the excitement that bubbled through her veins like champagne.

Leah didn't have a chance to speak with her godmother until they were in the carriage on the way home. Lady Wheaton started the conversation by saying, "You're bouncing like a kitten, child. I gather this is about Duncan Townley, since you shamelessly partnered him for two dances in a row."

"Am I that transparent?" Leah said with a laugh.

"It's one of your charms," her godmother said gently. "I'm continually amazed that a girl with your beauty is as direct and unaffected as you."

Leah's mouth twisted ruefully in the darkness. She was not sure that she deserved such a compliment, just as she felt that tributes to her beauty should go not to her but to the faery whose spell had created her appearance. But she could not say that to her godmother. "Captain Townley is a most attractive man," she said truthfully. "Tell me about him. I found that he has no wish to discuss his heroic deeds."

"Duncan is the nephew and heir of an old beau of mine, Viscount Townley," Lady Wheaton replied. "Though he was plain Will Townley then. We were quite infatuated for a time, but I wished to marry and he felt unready for such a commitment. So I accepted Wheaton, and Will went off to India. He was a great success there, I hear."

Wondering at the note she heard in her godmother's voice, Leah asked, "Are you still in love with Lord Townley, Aunt Andrea?"

"Nonsense," Lady Wheaton said briskly. "Wheaton was the most doting of husbands. I'm very attached to my stepchildren, and I have a comfortable income and the use of Wheaton House for the rest of my life. Altogether it was a most satisfactory marriage." Her voice softened. "Still, I do have fond memories of Will. I hear that he's recently returned from India, so I expect that eventually we'll see each other at some ball and laugh at just how young we once were."

To Leah, it seemed that perhaps her godmother protested a bit too much, but she did not pursue the point. "Have you known Duncan long?"

"Since his christening. His parents lived not far from us in the country."

Leah leaned forward in her seat eagerly. "What was he like?"

Lady Wheaton hesitated. "For all that he's so handsome and dashing, the word that comes to mind is—sweet. He was the most agreeable boy. Intelligent—he always had a book. Kind. Reliable. A little shy. But I haven't seen him since he came down from Cambridge. His parents died, and he went into the army and became that splendid masculine specimen that is coveted by every woman who sees him. He may be very different now from the boy I knew."

"Why is he considered a hero?"

"At Waterloo, the French tried to break through the line where his regiment was stationed. All of the senior officers were killed or wounded in the first assault, leaving young Duncan in command. Though he was wounded himself, his courage and leadership prevented the enemy from breaking the line."

Leah nodded, understanding better why he disliked the label hero. It had been bought at a very high price. Proceeding to the critical question, she asked, "His affections are unattached?"

"I believe so. As I said earlier, he has not been going about much in society. Dislikes being lionized, I believe. But I understand that he's been more visible in the last fortnight." Lady Wheaton laughed wickedly. "Good hunting, child. If you can't capture him, I don't know what woman could."

Leah leaned back, expression determined. This was why she had accepted a faery bargain for beauty—so she could win the heart of a man like Duncan Townley.

Even though mortals could not see him, from habit Ranulph stayed in the shadow of a massive rhododendron as he waited in the park opposite Wheaton House. As always, his Leah attracted an endless stream of male callers.

Then a smart sporting carriage drawn by matched bays swept into the square and halted in front of Wheaton House. The driver, a strikingly handsome young man of military bearing, gave his reins to his groom and jumped lightly to the ground, then entered the house. In a remarkably short time, he emerged with Leah on his arm. She was looking up into the man's eyes, her face bright with laughter.

She was exquisite, his little harpist. Ranulph greedily absorbed the sight of her slim, graceful figure and delicate features. He felt a surprising urge to reveal himself and wrench her away from her young man. Goddess, but he'd spent too much time observing mortals! He was developing some of their vices, such as jealousy.

He watched as the young man helped her into the carriage with tender care. Then the man left his groom to wait at Wheaton House, and drove off with Leah.

Ranulph scowled. He should be pleased. If he was any judge, his little harpist was finally well on her way to falling in love, which meant that the day when he could claim her was not far off. That knowledge only increased his impatience.

"Surely in London you can find other amusements while you wait to net your mortal miss," a familiar purring voice said.

Ranulph was becoming accustomed to Kamana's silent appearances. This time when he turned, his hand was not on the hilt of his sword. "There is enough greenery here to sustain faery life, but it is locked into strange, unnatural shapes. I shall be glad when the time comes to return to my wood." He suppressed a sigh. His longing for the familiar green peace as almost as powerful as his desire to have Leah there as his consort.

"It won't be much longer now," Kamana said. "The silver threads are crossing now, creating shared destinies. You'll be home again soon."

"I hope so." He studied her appreciatively. Today she wore an Indian costume that swathed her magnificent figure with provocative snugness. Necklaces of golden coins jingled around her neck and drew attention to her dark silky skin. "What are your London amusements, Lady Kamana?"

She shrugged, the gesture creating a tantalizing possibility that her wrapped garment would come unmoored. "Observing the passing scene. Visiting the green margins of the city. Did you know that near the river in Chelsea there is a wonderful apothecary's garden that contains plants from my own land?"

She gave a dazzling smile. "But mostly I watch these strange, intriguing mortal creatures."

"Surely you cannot wish to stay in London forever."

"Oh, no," she said positively. "Soon I shall return to the country. I've visited the great faery courts in Somerset and Derbyshire, and some smaller ones as well. I know what home I would prefer, but I will not speak of it until I'm sure I will be accepted."

He smiled down at her. For all her regal bearing, she was really quite a small creature. "I'm sure that whatever court you choose will welcome you gladly."

"We shall see." She pressed her hands together in front of her chest and bowed gracefully. "As we say in Hind, namaste. Until next time, Lord Ranulph."

She vanished in a shimmer of light. A good trick. He must learn how to do it. Then he turned and glided unseen through the street to Hyde Park so he could continue observing Leah and her mortal.

Leah enjoyed watching Duncan as he drove expertly through the crowded London streets. Heavens, she would enjoy watching him groom a horse or weed a garden! By the light of day he was every bit handsome as he had seemed last night. More so.

Yet she was even more struck by the quality that Lady Wheaton had mentioned the night before. Beneath the facade of a bold and dangerous-looking hero was a disposition of surprising sweetness. The expression in his golden eyes when he'd called for her had been almost shy.

Duncan had come at an unfashionably early hour so they would not be constantly interrupted by acquaintances. When they reached the park and the traffic no longer required his complete attention, he glanced at her and said, mirroring her own earlier thoughts, "You are even lovelier than I thought last night. Helen of Troy could not have surpassed you."

"That is a very pretty compliment," Leah said seriously. "But I would not want to launch a thousand ships. So much suffering! Not that I think it was Helen's fault. Surely Menelaus and Paris could have resolved their differences in a more civilized fashion."

Duncan grinned. "I've often thought the same. A duel would have been far more efficient. But the truth is that the Greeks simply liked to fight. I expect that any excuse would have done as well."

"Then they shouldn't have blamed the Trojan War on Helen," she said firmly. "It's the same as Adam blaming Eve for his own weakness. Most reprehensible."

He gave her a smile that made her knees weak. "I see that you are a radical."

"Not really, but I've read Mary Wollstonecraft Godwin and agree with much of what she said." Leah smiled ruefully. "I promised Lady Wheaton that I would not reveal my blue-stocking tendencies, but with you, I forgot my promise."

"I'm glad. Women with ideas are far more interesting than those who haven't two thoughts to rub together."

Leah glowed at his words. The compliment seemed to belong to her more than his praise for her beauty.

He continued, "Tell me about your family. Parents? Brothers and sisters?"

"No brothers and sisters," she said with regret. "I came late, when my parents had long since given up all thoughts of having a family."

"And...?" he said, perhaps hearing something in her voice.

She hesitated, then said aloud what she seldom admitted

even to herself. "My parents had little patience or interest in a child. They did their duty, of course, but..." Her voice trailed off before she continued, "Though my childhood was a quiet one, I always had my books and music. I was...content."

"I see," he said quietly, and she suspected that he did see.

"What of your family, Captain Townley?" she asked.

"Call me Duncan," he said with a warm look that reached deep inside her.

She seemed to be having trouble with her breathing. "Very well, Duncan. But...but you must call me Leah."

His answering smile was like a touch. How could the simple exchange of names feel so intimate?

"I was fortunate, for my parents were unfashionably interested in their offspring. I have two older sisters who alternately spoiled and tormented me." He grinned. "That's normal for families from what I've seen. Jane and Caroline are both married now. At last count I had five delightful nieces and nephews."

Trying not to sound too envious of his family, she asked, "Did you always wish to grow up and join the army?"

"Actually, my inclinations were scholarly rather than military." He concentrated rather more than necessary on steering around two stopped carriages. "But shortly after I finished at Cambridge, my parents died within a month of each other. I felt the need for a change." He smiled with wry self-mockery. "I also had romantic notions about serving my country, so I went into the army and was sent to the Peninsula just before the big push into France."

He'd had a baptism of fire. She did a swift calculation, and decided that he was only about twenty-five now. War had matured him early. "You may deny being a hero, but at the least, you served your country well," she said quietly. "Don't apologize for that."

He pulled his horses to a halt, then turned to her, the reins tight in his hands. "We both seem to have the ability to hear more than what the other person is saying."

So the deeper levels of this conversation were not in her imagination. She asked, "Is that bad?"

"No." He snapped the reins and set the horses into motion again. "Not bad at all."

For the rest of the drive, they talked about anything and everything. Leah had never found anyone, male or female, with whom she could converse so easily. And Duncan was obviously enjoying himself as much as she was. Could falling in love be this simple? She prayed that it was so.

As Duncan drove back to Wheaton House, he said with a touch of diffidence, "Tomorrow is the last night that Vauxhall will be open before closing for the winter. My uncle, with whom I'm staying, has suggested inviting you and your godmother to join us. Apparently she and my uncle are old friends. Might you be able to come?"

"Let me ask Lady Wheaton when we reach home. I believe we're free tomorrow night," she said, ruthlessly jettisoning invitations to three loud, crowded rout parties.

With a private smile, she guessed that her aunt would be almost as interested in the excursion as Leah.

CHAPTER 5

AFTER SPATTERING RAIN ALL DAY, the skies began to clear as dusk approached. Leah gave thanks—she did not want the evening at Vauxhall canceled. She was ready and bouncing with eagerness an hour before Lord Townley and Duncan were due to arrive.

Monique, who styled Leah's hair, shook her head sadly. "You must not wear your heart on your sleeve, M'zelle. Men like Captain Townley enjoy the hunt. Where is the challenge in a woman who falls into the hand like a ripe plum?"

Shadow, who was sitting on the vanity table with her paws tucked primly under her, gave a soft, scornful yowl. Feeling supported, Leah said, "Captain Townley is not like that. He would despise such games." She was not sure how she knew that, but she was quite positive that she was right.

After Monique left, still shaking her head, Leah stroked Shadow's luxuriant black fur. Now that she thought about it, she realized that the cat's eyes were the same transparent gold as Duncan's. An interesting coincidence.

She spent the next hour playing her harp, and wondering if Duncan would like the traditional instrument as much as he had enjoyed her piano playing. Wryly she recognized that every thought in her head involved Duncan one way or another.

When a maid summoned her, she raced down the stairs like a hoyden. Outside the drawing room, she made herself pause to take a deep breath. Then she went in.

Duncan greeted her warmly and made the introductions. Lord Townley was a lean, handsome gentleman with silver-touched hair and an unfashionably brown complexion. He bowed over her hand. "I had thought my nephew exaggerated your beauty, but I see that he understated the case!"

Leah liked the twinkle in the viscount's eye, and the obvious affection between him and his nephew. One of the bits of female advice that Lady Wheaton had offered was that a man who could get along with his relations was a good prospect for getting along with a wife. Leah had learned more such useful things in a few weeks with her godmother than in twenty-one years with her real mother.

Lady Wheaton swept grandly into the parlor, looking particularly fine in a navy blue costume trimmed in military-style gold braid. Lord Townley swung around, and there was a suspended moment while they looked at each other. Both of them were very still until the viscount said softly, "You haven't changed at all, Andrea."

To Leah's amazement, her worldly godmother blushed. "Nor have you, Will. You're still an outrageous flirt."

"A flirt?" he protested. "I'm a simple man, dedicated to the pursuit of truth."

"Hmph. The truth isn't in you," she said, but she took his arm eagerly when he offered it.

Leah and Duncan exchanged a glance of mutual surprise and amusement. As they followed the older couple out to the carriage, Duncan said under his breath, "I had thought my uncle a dedicated bachelor. But perhaps I was wrong."

Leah laughed and tightened her clasp on his arm. Magic was in the air. Why shouldn't Lord Townley and Lady Wheaton also feel the enchantment?

Ranulph had visited Vauxhall Gardens several times. During the day, the acres of trees were a welcome respite from the stone and stink of the city. He'd come several times at night as well. The concerts weren't bad, though nothing like as good as faery music, or the lilting airs that Leah played. But in the tree-shadowed paths, it was simple to find women who would lie with a handsome stranger. The physical satisfaction he'd found in such encounters was fleeting, but easily come by.

Tonight was different because Leah was here, along with her damned suitor. The young man was definitely a suitor—a blind man could see that.

Leah and her party had promenaded along the Grand Walk, watched the Cascade, and dined in a supper box. There was something afoot between the older man and Leah's godmother as well—Ranulph could see the energy glow between them. Not as intense as the radiant bond between Leah and young Townley, but definitely there, and growing stronger. The lot of them were having such a good time that they were like feasting court faeries, he thought acidly.

After the fireworks display, the couples separated and went off to promenade through the gardens, wanting privacy to talk—or for other reasons. Ranulph drifted through the shrubbery, watching Leah. The provocative sway of her hips as she walked intoxicated him. And her breasts, ah, those perfect little breasts....

He caught his breath as an idea struck him. What if a patch of fog rolled in from the river while Leah and her suitor were on the Dark Walk? No one would think anything of it. In the mist it would be easy to separate Leah from Townley. Lost and confused, she would run to her suitor in relief when she found him. Except that it would be Ranulph she would find, guised in the form of the man she desired.

He gave a great shout of laughter as the plan took form in his mind. He'd have her tonight, and pleasure her so well that she would be mad for the young man whose face he wore. Then, when her wits were scrambled with love, it would be time for Ranulph to collect his price, and she would be his.

In his bed—and in flower-filled glens and mossy bowers—he would bind her to him with the erotic arts learned over centuries, skills no mortal could hope to match. Through passion he would swiftly overcome any resentment she had at being compelled to leave the world of mortals. Not that he expected much resistance. Once she adjusted, how could she not prefer eons of pleasurable life in the glittering realms of Faerie?

He waited until Leah and her escort left the lighted Grand Cross Walk for the Dark Walk. Then, his gaze following her graceful figure, he raised one arm and summoned the fog.

Thick and soft as cotton wool, the dense mist rolled over the trees and walkways of this corner of the gardens, muffling sounds and reducing vision to a matter of two or three feet. Even Ranulph could see little.

All about him were gasps and feminine squeals of surprise. Ranulph smiled and snapped his fingers as he murmured a few words in the ancient tongue of magic. A spell of confusion formed in his palm, a dim sphere with dark swirling streaks inside. He tossed it toward Leah and Townley. The spell was a small one, and would affect only them and an area of fifty feet or so around.

Then, silent as the fog, he headed toward where he had last seen her. He'd done his work too well, for even he became confused. She was not where he expected, and neither was her escort. Ranulph stopped and searched the dense fog with scent and sound and intuition. Trees to the left, beyond that two people coupling, and not with the partners they'd come with. But where was Leah?

He heard light steps on the gravel path. A soft voice said uncertainly, "Duncan?"

Vibrant with excitement, he made himself visible to mortal eyes in the guise of Duncan Townley. He took a moment to familiarize himself with the new form. He had to admit that it was not a bad body, for a mortal. Then he called, "Here, Leah!"

He stepped forward, and almost ran into her. She gasped, "Oh!" as he caught her shoulders to steady her.

"Are you all right?" he asked, the words coming in a deep voice that was not his own. Slowly he ran his hands down her arms as he studied her delicate features.

She smiled, shamefaced. "I am now. I don't know quite how I lost you. One moment I had your arm. Then the fog came, and I became confused."

"I know. I was worried." He drew her into his arms and held her close. After making a small sound of surprise, she nestled close.

Reminding himself that he must go slowly, he kissed the top of her head, then gently moved his lips to her temple. She tilted her head back questioningly. The damp fog caused tendrils of hair to cling fetchingly to her throat. No longer able to restrain himself, he claimed her lips.

She gave a shiver of surprise. "I...I shouldn't," she whispered into his mouth.

"I was so worried," he said again, and kissed her bare throat, stroking her rapid pulse with his tongue.

Her mind might have doubts, but her body didn't. She pressed against him even as she murmured another vague protest. With a few steps he moved them to a mossy bed that he had created earlier, safely away from the graveled walk.

"This...this is most improper," she said weakly as he dropped to his knees, then tugged her down beside him.

"You're wrong," he said intensely. "For us, it's the most proper thing in the world." He started to say that he loved her, a phrase that worked like a magical spell on any mortal female who was already as aroused as Leah was. Yet he could not utter the words. In some indefinable way, it seemed wrong to lie to her about that.

He kissed her throat again, at the same time slipping her shawl from her shoulders and deftly unfastening the tapes securing the back of her gown. The bodice fell away, revealing her lacy underthings and the tops of her perfect breasts.

"Oh, Duncan." Eyes wide and startled, she made an ineffectual attempt to cover herself properly. "You really shouldn't do such things."

"I must have you, Leah," he said tightly. Though he wore the form of a mortal, it was Ranulph's own need that burned through his words. He captured her mouth, swallowing her protests while his hands delved beneath her gauzy garments.

He should have let his passion show sooner, for suddenly she was responding with a desire that matched his own, her small hands biting into his back. She was like a flame, her lithe body twisting beneath his, her hands and mouth eager.

Madness swept through him, a scorching need to make her his own. Yet even as he possessed her, their bodies joining with a wildness that seared his senses, he realized that something was wrong. *Something was wrong!*

He cried out at the same time as she, drowning in passion's inferno. In that same instant, as he felt the fierce heat of her response, his partner suddenly transformed. Her slight body became more voluptuous, her tawny hair turned into a tangle of silken tresses as black as night.

With shock and incredulous rage, he realized that it was not Leah but Kamana who lay beneath him, her shapely limbs twined around him and her golden eyes filled with wicked amusement. Violently he wrenched himself from her embrace. "Damn you!" he panted. "How dare you interfere with me!"

She laughed, unabashed, and rolled onto her side, propping her head up on one hand. Her clothing had vanished, leaving her naked except for the gossamer spill of her raven hair. "Why are you so angry? You seemed to be enjoying yourself." Her free hand drifted to her breast, where the mark of his teeth still showed. "I thought I played the innocent very well, until the end."

He flushed. "That is not the point. You had no right to deceive me."

Her brows arched. "Yet you had a right to deceive that child, to take the virginity that mortals prize so much? That would have been unkind." Her voice became husky. "I thought that you were in need of a diversion, so I sacrificed myself to that cause."

He snorted. "Sacrificed! You carried on like a she-panther. The marks on my back will not disappear quickly. Is that why you came to England, to find bolder lovers than the Folk of India?"

Her laughter pealed through the fog that enclosed their private glen. "Sexual congress is one of the great arts among my people. There are none in Angland that could match the sensual skill of one of my kind."

Seeing that he was on the verge of explosion, she added

kindly, "Oh, I admit that you are not without a certain talent in this area. With practice, and the teaching of a skilled partner, you might someday equal a lord of Hind." She stretched a hand lazily toward him, her fingers trailing sparkles of light.

Cursing, he leaped to his feet before she could touch him. "You witch! You were probably driven out by your own kind, and that is why you've come here to plague me."

She dropped her teasing manner. "Not at all. But I will not let you hurt that child wantonly. The fact that she is bound by the faery bargain she made does not mean she must be your prey now. Have patience, and you will soon have all that you desire."

"What I desire is to be free of you," he said viciously. Then he whirled into the fog as her laughter followed him.

One moment Leah was smiling at one of Duncan's remarks, and the next the thickest fog she had ever seen had fallen with amazing swiftness. She gasped and turned around, then realized that somehow she had let go of Duncan's arm. At first she was not alarmed, thinking that he must be within touching distance.

But he wasn't. He had vanished. She moved toward where he had been, or where she thought he had been, without success. Fear began to rise in her. The fog was uncanny, menacing. Struggling to contain her panic, she called, "Duncan?"

There was no answer. Hands clenched, she called again. Why could she hear nothing? It was as if she had fallen from the face of the earth into a nightmare.

Then she heard a faint, "I'm here, Leah."

She exhaled with relief, but in the fog it was impossible to tell from where his voice had come. Uncertainly she turned in a circle. "Where?" she called back.

"Stay where you are," he ordered, his voice a little closer. "If we both move, we'll never find each other."

Obediently she stood still, drawing her shawl tight against the biting chill. After what seemed like forever but was probably only a couple of minutes, Duncan emerged from the fog in front of her.

"Thank heaven!" She reached out with both hands.

He caught them, his grip warm and secure. "Are you all right?"

She nodded, ashamed of her fear. "Just a little disoriented."

His hands tightened on hers. "I had a strange feeling that there was some great danger in the fog. Danger for you. I was terrified that I wouldn't find you in time."

She swallowed. "I was afraid too, until you came."

He cupped her face in his hands, his gaze intense. "I don't know what I would do if something happened to you, Leah. I feel as if I've known you forever instead of just a few days."

"I...I feel the same way." Tears stung in her eyes, and she didn't know why.

"You are so lovely, Leah," he whispered. "The loveliest creature I've ever seen."

Then he bent his head and touched his lips to hers. The kiss was exquisitely gentle, totally different from the Duke of Hardcastle's rough embrace. But sweet, so sweet. She yearned toward him, feeling the effect of the kiss in every fiber of her body.

When he lifted his mouth away, she said shakily, "Is it wicked of me to enjoy that so much?"

"If so, we are wicked together." He wrapped her in a warm, protective hug. With a sigh she relaxed against him, feeling the beat of his heart. She was in love. Though she'd never experienced the state before, it was as unmistakable as a sunrise.

Duncan held her for long minutes, stroking her head and back. Finally he said reluctantly, "I must return you to your godmother before I do something I shouldn't."

She nodded, but didn't have the will to move away.

Slowly he disengaged himself from their embrace, his hands skimming over her back and hips as lightly as butterfly wings. "The fog should thin as we move away from the river," he said in a determined voice. "If we follow the gravel path, we'll be all right."

They set off, her hand locked in his. She counted her steps. Twenty. Fifty. A hundred. They walked out of the fog as abruptly as is they'd entered a lighted room. "How odd," Leah exclaimed, looking around at other revelers who were discussing the strange mist.

"Indeed," Duncan said thoughtfully. "Almost unnatural."

As they watched, the fog began to disperse almost as quickly as it had formed. Within a few minutes it was no more than a strange, dream-like memory.

Lord Townley and Lady Wheaton appeared from where the mist had lain, both of them looked pleased and suspiciously mussed. As the older couple came toward them, Duncan said swiftly, "May I call on you tomorrow? There is... something very important I want to discuss with you."

"Of course you may call," she said as her heart jumped. Might he be intending to offer for her? Though they hadn't know each other long, there seemed to be a rare harmony, a matching of minds and tastes, between them.

She hugged the possibility, knowing that she was grinning like a fool. She didn't care. She was in love, and she thought he loved her.

She had never been happier in her life.

CHAPTER 6

TOO NERVOUS TO EAT, Leah was glad that Lady Wheaton was abstracted at breakfast the next morning. Downright dreamy, in fact, with a smile hovering around her lips. She looked ten years younger and far less jaded than when Leah had first come to London.

Leah regarded her godmother fondly. If not for Lord Ranulph's magic, it was unlikely that the two women would have ever become acquainted. Now there was a bond between them that was warmer than what existed between Leah and her mother. She owed the faery lord a great deal.

For the first time in days, she wondered what he would want in return, but she felt too happy to worry about that. In olden times, favored servants were sometimes rented houses in return for a peppercorn a year, or something equally trifling. Lord Ranulph had said that he loved her music, and it was only the laws of his people that required him to exact a payment in return. No doubt his price would be like those peppercorn rents.

Unable to eat, Leah mangled a piece of toast and hoped that Duncan would call early. But he did not come until afternoon. She spent the morning playing the harp and thinking about the evening before. The memory of his kiss, and his embrace, caused tingling energy to flow through her body. In a very real sense, she felt truly alive for the first time. Perhaps that was what it mean to be in love.

It was a relief when a maid arrived to tell her that Captain Townley was waiting in the drawing room. Leah took a swift glance in her mirror. She looked beautiful. It had become hard to remember exactly the differences in appearance from before Ranulph had worked his spell, though she remembered with icy clarity how it felt to be so plain that she was almost invisible in her own life.

Leah felt a little sadness that Duncan would never have noticed her as she was before. Winning his regard this way seemed almost like cheating. But her beauty gave him pleasure, so she was more grateful than guilty.

After composing herself, she went downstairs to the drawing room, carefully leaving the door ajar for propriety's sake. Duncan was leaning casually against the mantelpiece. As she watched the sunlight define the chiseled planes of his face, Leah said involuntarily, "You're the most beautiful man I've ever seen."

Instead of being pleased or embarrassed, he became still as a statue. Then, releasing his breath in a sigh, he said, "I can't think of myself as beautiful."

"Would you prefer handsome? Dashing? Heroic? You are all of those things," she said, amazed by her own boldness. "I love looking at you."

"I'm not the man you think, Leah," he said with sudden vehemence. "I'm not a hero, not dashing, not at all out of the common way. I'm a plain man who likes books and country living and music, who merely did his duty as the situation demanded."

His golden eyes darkened. "The only thing special about me is how much I love you. Meeting you was like...like coming home. I know it's too soon, and that I should not speak to you before talking to your father. I know also that you are a jewel who should be gracing the finest society in Britain, and I can't give you that. But is it possible"—his voice wavered for an instant—"do you think that you could be happy sharing a quiet life with me?"

He really was shy, she realized with amazement, perhaps as shy as she herself. Overcome with tenderness, she said, "I would like nothing better, Duncan." She went to him and took his hands before saying haltingly, "I love you. A rational person might laugh at us both, but I feel that...that in you I've found the other side of myself."

He scanned her face with riveting intensity. "Would you love me if I were ugly, or if this scar was far worse, or if I had never been called hero?"

Recognizing how much he cared about her answer, she took time to think before saying slowly, "I love your kindness, your humor, the way you make me feel safe and cherished." She gave him a shy smile. "I love the person I am when I am with you. I think that would be true no matter what you looked like, and even if you had never been lionized by London society."

His smile was radiant and relieved. "Then I'll go into the country and speak to your father. Is there any chance that he might refuse to allow me to pay my addresses?"

"None at all. You are not only wonderful, but wonderfully eligible." She smiled teasingly. "I'll be getting the best of this bargain, you know."

His expression turned wry. "Never think that, Leah. If only you knew."

Leah bit her lower lip. "My parents dislike surprises. I

think it would be wise for me to go home first and prepare them for your visit."

"Good. That means that as soon as I have his permission, I can come to you and make a formal offer." His arms slid around her. "Oh, Leah, Leah..."

She went into his embrace gladly. "This is very forward of me, but I'd like the engagement to be short."

His laughter was rich and deep. "As short as we can decently make it."

She sighed with delight. It was hard to believe that such happiness could be real. As she rested against him, loving his warmth and strength, a dreadful thought struck her. Surely Ranulph couldn't ask for her first-born child! But there were ancient tales of faeries asking such a price.

The thought had not occurred to her when they had made their original bargain, probably because the idea of having a child was so far from her mind then. But it wasn't now. When she imagined marriage to Duncan, children were as much a part of the picture as Duncan himself. She would never give a child of theirs to a being who was as incomprehensible to her as the far side of the moon.

Surely her fears were pure, overwrought nonsense. Nonetheless, it was good that she was returning home now. She would find Ranulph and settle her debt. Then she could go into her new life freely.

Leah found it strange to be back in the bedroom she'd occupied since leaving the nursery. She'd changed so much, yet the room looked exactly the same. Well, the same except for Shadow, who had returned from London with her usual aloof dignity.

Her father had been bemused by Leah's announcement that a Captain Townley would be coming to speak with Sir Edwin on a matter of great import. However, he'd decided that he approved of the prospect after reading Lady Wheaton's letter that described Duncan's character and financial situation.

Rather sadly, Leah recognized that her parents would be glad to have her off their hands. Yet the knowledge didn't hurt the way it once had. As long as Duncan loved her, she could accept the fact that to her parents she was no more than a regrettable obligation.

On the morning after she arrived home, Leah slung her harp on her back and asked her dozing cat, "Would you like to come for a walk in the woods with me? There should be mice to chase and similar delights."

Shadow gave her mistress a look of contempt, then closed her eyes and swished her black tail over her nose. Leah chuckled. The cat was a good companion, but not over-interested in exertion.

It was a lovely autumn day, with a clear sky and pleasantly warm sunshine. Leah hiked into the woods to the glade where she had first met Ranulph. There she sat on the trunk of the fallen tree and played her harp. She sang of love and joy, and silently asked for the faery to come.

She'd almost given up hope when Lord Ranulph abruptly appeared in front of her, his golden hair drifting in the wind like thistle down. Leah caught her breath at the suddenness. This time he didn't wear the garb of a fashionable Englishman, but elegant garments of medieval cut, with a sword swinging at his side and dark hose that displayed the powerful muscles of his thighs. He was dangerously masculine, with an untamed light in his green eyes that made him seem far more alien than on their first meeting. But his tone was courteous when he bowed. "You wished to see, my lady."

Setting aside her harp, Leah stood and curtsied. "Your magic is strong, my lord. I went to London, as you arranged, and became very successful, as you predicted."

"I know," he said coolly. "I observed you in London myself."

She found the knowledge that he had spied on her disturbing. Had he eavesdropped on her private, tender moments with Duncan? She hated the idea.

Remembering his ability to read her mind, she tried to suppress the thought, but guessed from his cynical expression that he knew how she felt. She made herself smile. "I won the love of a hero, as you said I could. Soon I will be married. If it is agreeable to you, I would like to settle my debt now."

"Your timing is impeccable, Leah." He stalked across the clearing like a restless golden lion. "If you had not come here today, I would have summoned you."

Suppressing her uneasiness, she said, "You told me I would have three choices, my lord. What are they to be?"

"Can't you guess what I really want?" He stopped and turned to regard her with drugging eyes. "I want you to become my consort. I want you to live with me in Faerie, surrounded by music and beauty always. I will show you wonders such as you have never imagined. Come to me, Leah." He extended one long beautiful hand.

She felt the fierce power of his desire, the dark strength of his magic tugging at her. "No!" she said violently.

She retreated until the backs of her legs were pressed against the fallen tree. "I don't belong in your world, Lord Ranulph. I can't imagine how you could believe that I would ever agree to such a thing."

His up-tilted brows arched, and she saw that he was

laughing at her. "But you will, my dear girl. It is the best of the choices I offer you."

She ran her tongue over her dry lips. "Tell me the other two."

He began to pace around the glade again, his sword swinging by his side. "You say that you are to be married. Captain Townley, I assume." Ranulph gave her a glance that demanded a reply.

"Duncan and I have an understanding," she said reluctantly. "After he has spoken to my father, our betrothal will be official."

"A handsome youth," Ranulph said musingly. "A warrior hero."

Leah nodded warily, not sure where this was leading.

The faery lord halted at the far side of the clearing and turned to face her. In a voice that chilled her to the bone, he said, "Your second choice, my dearest girl, is to bring me his heart."

Leah stared at Ranulph. "What do you mean? The fact that he has pledged me his heart does not mean that I can give it to another. Love isn't like that!"

The faery's eyes narrowed. "I was not speaking in metaphor, Leah. Never fear, I shall make the task easy." A silver dagger materialized in his hand, the blade glittering wickedly. "This is an enchanted blade. Even a small creature like you will find it easy to slide the dagger between his ribs and cut out his heart when he is dead."

"You're mad!" Shocked beyond words, she gagged, on the verge of vomiting at the horrific image conjured by Ranulph's words. To look into Duncan's smiling eyes, then murder him... She pressed her hand to her mouth as her stomach heaved.

Bland as butter, Ranulph continued, "I suggest that you do the deed when on a walk in my wood, so you will not have to go far to deliver your payment. You need not fear retribution from your own kind. Simply weep prettily and claim that you were set upon by a madman who slew your lover. No one will believe that a woman so beautiful, so fragile, so in love, could perform such a bloody deed."

He smiled satirically. "After a suitable mourning period, you will be free to seek another husband. That duke who mauled you in his garden, for instance. He was angry then, but I'm sure you could win him back with a single enchanting smile." Ranulph pressed the silver dagger into her numb hand. The hilt was cool against her palm.

She stared at the shining weapon, her horror intensifying. "I can't. I *won't!*"

He tilted his head, wicked, inhuman amusement in his eyes. "I didn't think you would. That's why I waited until now. It would take a fierce woman to kill her lover."

"You needn't have waited so long," she said in a shaking voice. "I could never do such a thing even to a stranger."

"You are that sentimental about all mortals?" he said, surprised. "If I had realized the extent of your squeamishness, I would have come to claim you sooner."

More than anything else he had done, that statement made Leah realize how utterly alien he was. He simply had no understanding of humans. "What is your last choice, my first born child?" she said bitterly. "If you ask that, I swear I shall use your dagger right now." She raised the weapon in shaking hands and held it to her breast, wondering if she would have the strength to kill herself. He'd said the blade was enchanted. Perhaps it would slide home easily...

Ranulph leaped across the clearing in one bound and wrenched the dagger away from her. "Goddess, and you think *I'm* insane?" he said furiously. "I don't want your life, nor another man's squalling brat."

He tossed the dagger aside. It vanished in mid-air. More calmly, he said, "A babe fathered by me—now that would be more interesting. The Folk are not prolific, but in an eternity of mating, we are bound to produce a child now and then."

He truly intended to own her body and soul. Shaking her head in revulsion, Leah said, "You owe me another choice, Lord Ranulph. Whatever it is, it cannot be as evil as what you have already suggested."

He smiled at her, as splendid and amoral as a wild beast. "Your last choice is not evil at all. Such a simple thing."

She laced her trembling hands together. "Don't play with me, my lord," she said tightly. "Just tell me what you want."

"A simple thing," he repeated. "But, I think, the highest price of all. If you decline the other choices, it will cost you your beauty."

CHAPTER 7

LEAH STARED AT RANULPH, her eyes wide and shaken. "My beauty?"

He winced inwardly at her distress, but it was necessary. He'd set the order of the choices deliberately, knowing that her first reaction to leaving her own kind would be refusal. Only after hearing all the choices would she take his proposal seriously.

Careful to keep all sympathy from his voice, he said coolly, "Don't play the fool, Leah. Refuse me, and you'll become again the plain creature you were before. Dull and colorless, almost invisible. Most people will not really understand the change, though anyone who saw you during your London triumphs will have trouble remembering why he thought you such a great beauty then."

His voice dropped. "But your suitor will remember. He'll look at you with shock and revulsion. How many times did Captain Townley praise your beauty? How often did he murmur in your ear about your loveliness? When your beauty vanishes, so will his love. You will live the rest of your life alone and despised."

He gave a bored shrug. "I suppose that since masculine honor is involved, you may be able to hold him to the betrothal. In that case, you will have the pleasure of living with a man who despises you for deceiving him."

Her eyes, an emerald mirror of his own, filled with tears until she closed them. Her exquisitely expressive face revealed that she was imagining exactly what Ranulph had described: rejection by her lover, a return to her empty existence.

Judging it time to change his tactics, he said softly, "Now do you understand why I said that becoming my consort was the best choice? Come with me and I shall give you passion and beauty beyond your wildest imaginings. Great caves shimmering with secret jewels. Forests with a majesty that would humble the greatest human cathedral. We'll ride the wind and sing the seas, and you shall never regret your decision!"

Confident that the web of words he'd spun would change Leah's mind, he stepped forward and took her hand between both of his. Goddess, but she was lovely! He felt himself hardening with desire. Passion would sweep away the last of her doubts.

He drew her into a kiss. Her mouth was soft, her scent as fresh as spring flowers. He used all his erotic skills, he focused all his desire, weaving a spell that would leave her begging for more.

But it didn't work. She tore herself away, wiping her mouth with the back of her hand in revulsion. "Do you think I could ever prefer your touch to that of Duncan?" She lifted her harp and clutched it like a talisman against harm. "Perhaps you can cloud my mind with magic, but I will never be your whore voluntarily!"

He stared at her, shocked that she could resist his sensual spell. Who would have thought that she had such strength? Then he produced his magic mirror with a snap of his fingers and held it up as a reminder of what she had looked like. Ruthlessly he used an image of her at her worst, with her eyes swollen and her nose pink from crying. "Is this what you choose?" he said cruelly. "Or will it be your lover's heart?"

She paled at the image in the mirror, but said resolutely, "Return me to what I was, Lord Ranulph. I was plain all of my life. I...I can learn to be plain again."

"You don't know what you're saying!" he exclaimed, incredulous. "It was bad enough to have no looks before, but now you have known the delights of beauty. The adoration, the power, the fame. To lose those things after briefly tasting them will be infinitely more painful than never to have known them."

"Do you think I don't know that?" she cried out, clutching the harp even tighter. "But I can bear it. I shall have to, since both your other choices are unthinkable. I could never harm Duncan, nor any other innocent. Nor can I give up my whole world to become the slave of a creature who is as beautiful and alien as a tiger."

"I want you for my consort, not my slave!" he snapped in a voice like a whip.

"Isn't it slavery if I go against my will?" Her mouth twisted. "You and I are made of different stuff, Lord Ranulph. You think beauty more valuable than freedom, more precious than another person's life. I can no more understand that than you can understand me. Good-bye, my lord. I presume that by the time I reach my home, I will be plain again, and our bargain will be fulfilled."

She slipped away from him and headed across the glade. Before entering the woods, she paused to say quietly, "I...I'm sorry that I cannot be what you wish."

Stunned that she was really leaving, for an instant he stood frozen. Then he gave a wild shout of anger. *"No!"*

He flung both arms to the heavens, and thunder boomed from the clear autumn sky, rolling across the wood with a force that shook the trees. Leah flinched, and he saw alarm in her eyes.

Realizing that if she feared him all hope was gone, he said tightly, "I shall not harm you, Leah. Not now, not ever. If ever you become disenchanted with being plain and lonely and despised, you know how to summon me."

She gave a faint nod of her head, but he knew with despair that she would never change her mind. Except for her music, she was as much a mystery to him as he was to her. Was that because she was a mortal, or simply because she was female?

Saturated with pain, he watched her disappear among the trees. She was gone, and he was alone.

Then rage returned. With a gesture of his hand, he removed the faery glamour that had dazzled all of London. Viciously he contemplated how her lover would react to the discovery that his ravishing betrothed was now as plain as a barn mouse.

The restless churn of his anger turned toward Kamana. *Damn* the treacherous female! Her predictions that Leah would come to him were empty, more of her mocking games. She would answer to him for her lies. She had power, but he was her equal. She would be unable to refuse if he summoned her.

He closed his eyes and visualized Kamana until her exotic, teasing image was burned in his brain. Then he uttered the words of Power that would bring her to him, against her will if necessary.

She'd pay for her interference and lies, the traitorous witch. Aye, she'd pay!

Leah was still shaking when she reached home. Not wanting anyone to see the tears on her face, she crept up the back stairs and into her bedroom.

Shadow still lay on the bed. At Leah's entrance, the cat opened her eyes and gazed at her fixedly. Leah tried to smile. "Don't tell me that you'll abandon me, too. I would have thought that at least my cat would accept me as I am now."

Shadow leaped from the bed and came to rub Leah's ankles, purring warmly. A little comforted, Leah scratched the cat's neck.

Then she turned to her mirror. Any faint hope she'd harbored that Ranulph might not exact his price died. Drab hair, thin figure, ordinary gray-green eyes reddened from tears. She glanced at her left palm. In the center, she could still see the faint iridescent glimmer of the cut Ranulph had made when they'd sealed their bargain. Apparently it would be the only lasting sign of what she had been.

She inhaled painfully and forced herself to stare at her reflection. Had he made her uglier than before, or did her appearance seem worse because of the contrast to what she had been? No matter. This was the face she was born with, and would die with. She reminded herself that she'd had no real choice. Murder was unthinkable, and so was going into whatever strange, inhuman netherworld Ranulph called home.

She winced as she remembered Duncan's worshipful gaze, the number of times he'd told her that she was the most beautiful creature he had ever seen. He was too much a gentleman to break his pledged word when he saw what she had become, but Ranulph was right. It would be even worse to live with Duncan and know that he despised her than to live without him. She must release him from the betrothal.

The thought of losing him shattered her last shreds of composure. She threw herself onto the bed, sobbing uncontrollably. Shadow followed and touched her cool nose to Leah's cheek, but that did nothing to allay the pain. Merciful heaven, Leah would have been better off if she'd never met Ranulph of the Wood, or if she had been wise enough to refuse his damnable bargain!

Or would she? She rolled onto her side and cradled the cat's warm, fluffy body. The cost of Ranulph's bargain had been bitterly high, but she had learned what it was to be beautiful, and that beauty was not an unalloyed blessing. She wouldn't miss the hungry stares of strangers, or the resentment of other woman.

Nor would she miss the endless balls and parties. After the first excitement of being admired had worn off, she'd realized that she was simply not a very sociable creature. She preferred a country life with her music and a small circle of friends, and would no longer yearn for the delights of London.

And Ranulph's bargain had allowed her to learn the joy of loving. Someday, when the anguish lessened, she would be glad of that.

But now the wound was still too raw. She buried her face in Shadow's silken fur and wept.

Exhausted by tears, Leah dozed. She was jerked awake when one of the housemaids tapped at her door. "Miss Leah, there's a fine young gentleman called Captain Townley here to see you!" the girl called through the door. She giggled. "He's just spoken to your father. Is there going to be an announcement?"

Leah pushed herself upright with a gasp of shock. Dear Lord, Duncan had already arrived and asked her father for her hand! She had thought he wouldn't come until tomorrow at the earliest. But he was impatient, as she had been.

She raked her fingers through her hair. She couldn't possibly see him like this. In fact, perhaps it would be best to write him a note. She'd apologize profusely and say that after serious consideration she had decided that they would not suit.

An image appeared in her mind of what his expression would be when he read such a letter. She realized that Shadow was staring at her, disapproval in the great golden eyes. The cat was right. It would be unforgivable to take the coward's way out and leave Duncan to a lifetime of wondering what had gone wrong. When he saw her, his love would evaporate painlessly, leaving him free of the misery that tormented her. She could find some small solace in that.

"Miss Leah?" the maid called again. "Aren't you in there?"

"Ask Captain Townley to wait in the morning room," Leah replied in a strained voice. "I'll be down in a few minutes."

She went to her washstand and splashed her face with cold water to reduce the redness. For pride's sake, she would look no worse than absolutely necessary. Luckily, her apple green gown was very pretty, one of her London acquisitions, and it made the best of her slight figure and fair complexion. Her hair was a disaster, so she combed it out and tied it back simply with a green ribbon, leaving it soft around her face.

Shadow was watching again. In her mind, Leah heard the words *Beauty is as much confidence as it is physical perfection.*

Leah blinked, realizing that was true. Lady Wheaton was not a classic beauty, but her graceful posture and confidence always made heads turn when she entered a room. Leah had carried herself differently after she'd become accustomed to her faery beauty.

Remembering how she had felt when she made an entrance and known that all eyes were on her, she raised her head proudly. She would not hold Duncan against his will, and she would not weep in front of him.

Farewell. Shadow was suddenly next to Leah, the golden eyes somber.

Leah swallowed hard at this unexpected loss. "I'm going to lose you, too, aren't I? You came with Ranulph's magic, and now you must leave since it is gone."

Sorrowfully she lifted the cat for a last hug. As she did, the image of a kitten appeared in her mind. A playful black kitten who would dance into Leah's heart, and soon. The knowledge was some comfort, though Leah knew there would never be another cat like Shadow.

After setting Shadow on the bed, Leah opened the casement, though if the cat was of Faerie, she probably didn't need an open window to leave. Then Leah headed toward the door. With black humor, she told herself that Duncan would be lucky to escape her, since clearly a woman who held imaginary conversations with her cat was half mad.

As she left the room, she felt a comforting warmth in her mind, almost like a purr.

Since the morning room faced east, it was dim this late in the day. Leah entered to find Duncan standing in front of the window, his broad-shouldered form a dark silhouette. Even when he turned, his features were too shadowed for her to read. That was a small mercy, she decided. "Good day, Duncan."

"Leah." He bowed, but didn't come to her.

Her heart died a little when she saw the ominous rigidity in his figure. He must be shocked by her drab appearance. She halted in the middle of the room, reminding herself to keep her head high. She could not change her looks, but she could at least behave with dignity. "You've spoken with my father?"

"Yes, and he gave his blessing willingly. But"—Duncan hesitated, then said in a rush of words—"before I make a formal offer, there is something I must say."

Suddenly desperate to speak first so that she needn't hear his confused, embarrassed questions, she said lightly, as if it was a matter of no importance, "No need to say anything. It's perfectly obvious that it was a mistake for us to consider marriage." Her gaze slid away and she blinked back tears. "Farewell, Captain Townley. I enjoyed our...flirtation."

She glided toward the door and was on the verge of escape when Duncan darted across the room and caught her arm. This close, she could see his shocked expression as he said, "Please don't go! At least, not yet." He swallowed hard. "I...I understand that you do not wish to marry me. I'm sorry, Leah. I warned you that I was not the man you thought. A woman as beautiful as you deserves so much more. But I, too, shall treasure our...flirtation."

She stared at him. "'A woman as beautiful as me?' Duncan, look at me! I'm as plain as a fence post. People would laugh at you for taking such an ill-favored wife when you can have any woman in England."

His gaze ran over her. "You do look a little less spectacular than usual today, probably from worrying how to tell me that you prefer to end our understanding. I'm sorry this has been so difficult for you." His voice roughened. "But even upset, you're still the loveliest sight I've ever seen, Leah. I...I shall never forget you."

The sincerity in his voice shocked her. If he still thought she was beautiful, it was because the room was too blasted dim. Grimly accepting that she must reveal herself in all her plainness, she took a candle from the table and thrust it into the small coal fire, then ignited a whole branch of candles so that light blazed over her.

She turned to Duncan. "You're wondering what happened to the girl you wanted to marry," she said flatly. "It's quite an interesting tale, though hard to believe. At the end of the summer, I met a faery who offered to make me beautiful for a price to be paid later."

She smiled without humor. "Not only was I made beautiful, but the thought was planted in Lady Wheaton's head that she'd like to present me, and presto! I was off to London. Excellent magic, wasn't it?" She shrugged with elaborate unconcern. "But the faery and I couldn't reach an agreement on the payment, so my beauty was revoked. It would be impossible to believe such a tale, except that the truth is written on my face."

He frowned. "Kamana came to you also?"

"Kamana?" Leah said, perplexed.

"The faery." Wearily he raked a hand through his brown hair. "She told me at the beginning that the change in my appearance could only be temporary. I knew you and I could not become betrothed until you had seen me as I really am, so yesterday I asked Kamana to remove her spell. She did so with a snap of her fingers, then told me not to worry, that all would be well. I didn't believe her, and rightly so. A woman with your beauty and charm deserves the very best, not an ordinary man like me."

Leah studied him, looking for changes in his appearance. Now that she looked, she could see that his eyes were no longer golden, but a pleasant hazel with flecks of green, and his hair had gone from near-black to medium brown. Though he was still broad-shouldered and fit, the dashing and dangerous aura that had drawn women like honeybees was gone. Yet he was still unmistakably Duncan.

Perplexed, she said, "The faery who came to me was male, Ranulph of the Wood. He dwells right here on my father's land, I think. Could he have transformed himself into a female to speak to you?" Even as she said the words, she rejected them. Ranulph was too wholly masculine to ever take the form of a woman.

Equally perplexed, Duncan said, "Kamana is from India. She came to England on the ship that carried my uncle and a hold full of plant specimens. After Waterloo, when I was recovering from my wounds, she appeared and said that my uncle had saved her life. In return, he'd asked that I be protected in battle."

Duncan gave a lopsided smile. "She apologized for not being able to turn aside all harm, but her spell surely preserved my life and caused me to heal quickly. You see why I should not be called a hero? Because of my uncle's good deed, I was protected from the guns that killed my comrades. I deserve no credit for that."

So that was the source of his self-deprecation. "Nonsense!" Leah said vehemently. "Did you know during the battle that you were protected?"

When he shook his head, she continued, "Then how does a faery spell diminish your deed? As far as you knew at the time, you could die at any instant, as your friends had. It wasn't magic that rallied your regiment and stopped the French advance. It was your courage and skill. Your heroism, Duncan."

As she scanned his beloved face, trying to infuse him with her belief, she recognized that he had been wounded more gravely than she had known. She went to him and tenderly touched the rough scar that ran from his temple to the middle of his cheek. This was not the thin line that had seemed like an elegant accessory to the dramatic good looks of a drawing room hero, but the mark of a savage injury that might have taken his life. "To me, you will always be a hero," she said quietly.

He flinched away from her fingers. "Ugly, isn't it? In hospital, I couldn't even face myself in the shaving mirror. And there are a dozen more scars in less obvious places." He swallowed hard. "When Kamana came to me, she insisted on granting me a season of faery glamour so that I would not hide from society. Perhaps it would have been better if I had not agreed to that, for her magic merely delayed the time when I must come to terms with my disfigurement."

His voice softened. "Yet if not for Kamana's spell, I would never have met you, much less had the courage to speak, or...or to kiss. I cannot regret that."

"You're not ugly," Leah said vehemently. "Even without faery glamour, you're the most attractive man I've ever known, Duncan. I love the way you look, just as I love your strength and kindness and conversation and a thousand other things about you."

A startling thought struck her. If she loved Duncan even though he was not the dashing, Byronic hero who had made half of London swoon, there was a chance that he might love her even though she was not beautiful.

She took a deep breath, then asked hardest question of her life. "Do...do you think you could care for me even though I am plain?"

Amazed, he said, "How can you think yourself plain? Though you don't glitter quite as much, you are still enchantingly slim and graceful, with a smile that lights up the room and eyes as warm as a winter fire. Beautiful! At least, you are beautiful to me."

He cupped her cheek tenderly. "As I told you once before, when we met I felt I had come home," he said in a husky voice. "Now that we see each other truly, I love you even more than before."

Laughing with joy, she went into his arms. How foolish she had been to think that love was only about surfaces, and that no man could love her unless she matched some impossible ideal of perfection. "Duncan, Duncan, I love you so!"

They came together in a fierce embrace. As Leah raised her face for his kiss, she gave passionate thanks for the miracle of having found the other half of herself.

CHAPTER 8

RAGING, Ranulph stalked about the glade until Kamana appeared before him in a blaze of light. Magnificent and terrible, she wore an Indian garment of scarlet silk that brilliantly emphasized her dark, sultry skin and the raven hair that swirled around her.

"You summoned me, Lord Ranulph?" she said with cool composure.

He scowled at her. "Time and again you interfered with my pursuit of Leah. Today she rejected me, despite your assurances that she would be mine!" His voice turned to ice. "You influenced her, didn't you? Perhaps even bespelled her so that she could resist my magic. Why, damn you? What have I done that you take such pleasure in thwarting me?"

"I never said that Leah would accept you, Ranulph. Only that your destined consort would soon be yours, and that is the truth." Kamana glided toward him, her figure swaying provocatively and her bare feet scarcely bending the autumn grass. "Why do you think I came halfway around the world? Destiny, my lord!"

She was taunting him again. Furiously he wrapped his

hands around the warm flesh of her throat, wanting to see her fear, wanting her to plead for mercy.

Kamana laughed at him, her slanting eyes glowing like new-minted coins. "Is the thought of me as your consort that terrible, Ranulph? I thought our encounter in the park was rather pleasing."

"You mocked me then, and you mock me now," he growled. His fingers tightened until he could feel the hammer beat of her pulse beneath his thumbs. "If we were really destined mates, why not simply say so?"

"You're a stubborn creature," she replied calmly. "All your thoughts and dreams were centered on that mortal child. How would you have reacted if I'd announced that you and I were fated to be together?"

She was right again, damn her. His hands dropped and he stepped back. "I'd have said I'd sooner mate with a hedgehog than share my life with you!" he snarled.

"You shall find me a much better companion than a hedgehog." She tossed her head, her silken hair shimmering like an ebony veil. "You cannot fight fate, Ranulph. Come, I have something to show you."

Kamana crossed the clearing to where a rivulet of water formed a small pool before trickling away. She waved her hand, and an image of Leah and her young man appeared in the water. They were sitting side by side on a sofa. Townley said something and Leah laughed, turning to rest her forehead against his shoulder as she laid her hand lightly on his chest. His arm came around her, and he kissed her soft temple.

Ranulph saw the tenderness, and ached inside. "Are you saying that mortals, with their short lives and eternal souls, are more fortunate than the long-lived, soulless Folk?"

Kamana gave him a glance of mild exasperation. "All things that live are formed of spirit, Ranulph. The trees around us, the grass beneath us, all creatures great and small. That includes the Fair Folk, so I'll hear no more talk of our lacking souls."

His gaze went back to the image of the two young mortals. They were kissing now, and Leah was beautiful. Beautiful in a quiet, far more profound way than the dazzling faery glamour that Ranulph had granted her.

"Those two are soul twins, which is why their love could not be affected by faery spells," Kamana explained. "When Duncan's uncle asked me to protect the boy, I traced the thread of his destiny, and found that without magical aid, he would die at Waterloo."

She shook her head with regret. "Despite my best efforts, he was injured in body, and even more in spirit, on that terrible day. The physical wounds were not hard to heal, but an injured spirit is much harder. When I looked again at his destiny line, I realized that the best remedy would be to bring him to Leah. Ordinarily it would have taken them longer to come together, longer still to realize that they were true mates. But because you and I had touched them with faery magic, they both sensed their fate almost instantly."

"It sounds to me as if you interfered with their so-called destiny," Ranulph said with heavy sarcasm.

"I was merely an instrument of fate, a way of bringing them together. The same is true of these two." She gestured and a new image showed in the pool. Lord Townley and Lady Wheaton were also on a sofa, but the activity they were involved in was nowhere near as innocent as mere kissing. Ranulph's gaze sharpened with interest at the sight of the tumbled skirts and passionate movements, but before he could get a clear look Kamana waved away the image.

"Lord Townley asked nothing for himself, but I thought I would speed him toward the secret wish of his heart," Kamana explained. "My aid was not essential. I merely helped him recognize his destiny sooner."

Exotic and beautiful, Kamana gazed at Ranulph with slanting eyes that had seen mysteries half a world away. She was so alluring that he almost reached out to draw her to him. Instead, he retreated, scowling. "So you went to London as a spy!"

She grinned. "Indeed I did." There was a shimmer of light, and the faery was replaced by a large black cat with long silky hair and golden eyes the same shade as Kamana's. Purring, the beast rubbed against his ankles in sensual invitation.

He had to smile. Scooping the cat up in his arms, he said, "You're an excellent shape shifter." Still purring, the creature settled into the crook of his arm. Ranulph stroked the soft furred belly, thinking that a cat might be a good companion in the lonely nights of winter.

Suddenly Kamana returned to her own form and he was holding a glorious, half-naked female in his arms. She was warmly alive and scented with the rare perfumes of Araby, and his hand was on her full, silk-clad breast.

Throatily she said, "Shape shifting isn't all that I'm good at." Her hand slid down his body, arousing him with indecent ease.

Furious at how cleverly she manipulated him, he dropped her like an armful of burning timber. As she gave an acrobatic twist in mid-air that landed her on her feet, he snapped, "You said that I was carnally unskilled compared to the Folk of your land! Why would you want to mate such a clumsy creature as I?"

"There is more to mating than mere technique." Her eyes gleamed wickedly. "You're quite arrogant enough already. I didn't want to feed your vanity by saying that never had I known such passion, or such satisfaction."

"But *why?*" He caught her shoulders, trapping her so that she must look at him. "Why me? Why risk a journey halfway around the world to become the consort of a stranger?"

She became utterly still, her gaze locking with his. "Because of who and what you are, Ranulph," she said quietly. "Our people mate often, but seldom love. Few of the Folk desire the kind of bond you wanted to have with Leah."

She raised her hand to his face, her fingers light. "You were mistaken in your choice of mate, but not in the truth of your heart. You have a rare capacity to love, Ranulph, though it is a word the Folk never use."

Kamana closed her eyes for a moment. When she opened them again, she let him see into her soul, to the vulnerability and desperate yearning that she hid behind her teasing. "I wanted love, but could not find it in my own land. Like you, I was a solitary who yearned for my true mate. I spun a great and dangerous spell to find if such a being even existed. In the vision that followed, I saw a wild and golden faery lord who lived in a far distant place. I knew then that my true mate existed, though to find you I would have to risk my very existence. But if I succeeded, the silver threads of our destinies would knot and become one forever."

Her eyes searched his, uncertainty and hope in the golden depths. "I thought I recognized you the moment we first met. Was I wrong? Did...did I allow my yearning to distort my vision?"

In the drowning pools of her eyes, he saw an end to loneliness, a craving for union that matched his own. He'd never found such longing among the Folk of his land, had not believed that it existed anywhere except among humankind. That was why he had become obsessed with Leah, because he'd known that the mortal girl had an immense capacity to love.

With wonder and deep humility, he recognized the rare and precious gifts Kamana was offering. Companionship. Passion. A love for all eternity. This was what he had longed for, this shining creature from a far place who knew the shape of his spirit, and would complete it with her own.

Huskily he said, "No, Kamana. You were not wrong." Then, with a blossoming of joy, Ranulph drew her into his arms, and surrendered to his destiny.

~

And they all lived happily ever after.

AUTHOR'S NOTE

THANK you for taking the time to read *Beware Faery Gifts*. I hope you've enjoyed it—and if so, please consider helping other readers find it by leaving a review of the book at your favorite online bookstore or reader website.

Also, if you would like me to let you know when my upcoming books are published, you can join my newsletter at MaryJoPutney.com.

Happy reading!
—Mary Jo Putney

ALSO BY MARY JO PUTNEY

Silk and Secrets, #2
Veils of Silk, #3
Christmas Silks: A Silk Trilogy Novella

Other Historicals
Lady of Fortune
Dearly Beloved
Uncommon Vows
The Rake
The Bargain
The Marriage Spell (paranormal)

Putney Classics (Sweet Regency Romances)
The Diabolical Baron
Carousel of Hearts

The Lackland Abbey Chronicles
(Young Adult fiction, written as M. J. Putney)
Dark Mirror, #1 (includes a bonus Lackland short story)
Dark Passage, #2
Dark Destiny, #3

The Guardian Trilogy
(Historical fantasy, written as M.J. Putney)
A Kiss of Fate, #1
Stolen Magic, #2
A Distant Magic, #3
Unseen Magic: A Guardian Novella

The Lost Lords Series
Loving A Lost Lord, #1
Never Less Than A Lady, #2
Nowhere Near Respectable, #3

No Longer A Gentleman, #4
Sometimes A Rogue, #5
Not Quite A Wife, #6
Not Always a Saint, #7

Rogues Redeemed Series (A Spin-Off of the Lost Lords)

Once A Soldier, #1
Once a Rebel, #2
Once A Scoundrel, #3
Once A Spy, #4
Once Dishonored, #5
Once A Laird, #6

The Circle of Friends Trilogy

The Burning Point, #1
The Spiral Path, #2
An Imperfect Process, #3
A Holiday Fling: A Circle of Friends Novella (also published in *Christmas Revels*)

Shorter Works

One Wicked Winter Night (a Christmas novella)
The Dragon and the Dark Knight (written as M.J. Putney)
Beware Faery Gifts (written as M.J. Putney)
Weddings of the Century: A Pair of Novellas
The Best Husband Money Can Buy (novella, also published in *Christmas Candles*)
Mad, Bad, and Dangerous To Know (novella, also published in *Christmas Candles*)
The Christmas Cuckoo (novella, also published in *Christmas Revels*)
The Black Beast of Belleterre (novella, also published in *Christmas*

Revels)
Sunshine for Christmas (novella, also published in *Christmas Revels)*
The Christmas Tart (novella, also published in *Christmas Revels)*

Christmas Collections
Christmas Revels
Christmas Candles
Mischief and Mistletoe (contributor)
The Last Chance Christmas Ball (contributor)
Christmas Roses (contributor)
Seduction on a Snowy Night (contributor)
A Yuletide Kiss (contributor)

ABOUT THE AUTHOR

~

A *New York Times, Wall Street Journal,* and *USA Today* bestselling author, Mary Jo Putney a.k.a M.J. Putney is also a recipient of RWA's Nora Roberts Lifetime Achievement Award. She was born in Upstate New York with a reading addiction, a condition for which there is no known cure. Her entire romance writing career is an accidental byproduct of buying a computer for other purposes.

Her novels are known for psychological depth and intensity and include historical and contemporary romance, fantasy, and young adult fantasy. Winner of numerous writing awards, including two RITAs and two *Romantic Times* Career Achievement awards, she's had a number of her books listed as top romances of the year by *Library Journal* and *Booklist,* the magazine of the American Library Association.

Her favorite reading is great stories, but in a pinch she'll settle for the backs of cereal boxes. She's delighted that e-publishing can now make available books that have been out of print.